EVIDENCE OF A COMMUTER TRAIN

STANLEY B. TRICE

This book is a work of fiction. Names, characters, places, and incidents are the product of the author's imagination or used fictitiously. Any resemblance to actual events, places, or persons is coincidental.

Copyright © 2021 by Stanley B. Trice
Published by Every Word Rise, LLC
Place of Publication: New Bern, NC

Cover design by Natalia Junqueira via www.Reedsy.com
Formatting by Woven Red Author Services, www.WovenRed.ca

All rights reserved. No part of this publication may be stored in a retrieval system, reproduced, or transmitted by any means electronic, mechanical, photocopying, recording, or otherwise without prior written permission from the author.

Library of Congress Control Number: 2021909963

ISBN Ebook: 978-0-9909265-3-5
ISBN Print book: 978-0-9909265-2-8

Table of Contents

Boxcars 5
Phil Meets Angie 16
Angie's Hope 26
Tony Breathes 38
Who's Listening? 60
The Bathroom on the Train 67
The Back of the Seat 76
Commuting Agendas 83
Carolyn and Beatrice 92
Morning Commute 102
Incident on Train 302 112
wake up wake up 122
Running Out of Diesel 132
Clyde is as Big as a Hero 143
Sudden Stops 152
Clyde's Hunger 162
Paula and Betty 172
Voyages Home: A Week on the Commuter Train 183
Angie and Phil 201
Train Commuter Waiting 213
About the Author 219

Boxcars

The Commuter stood on the train station platform, exposed to the cold and descending darkness, and wanting to go home. Except his train was late. He waited along with his fellow commuters watching, on the far track, a hot shot freight train pass. Being a hot shot gave it a priority over other train traffic, and it was using that priority to take its time passing on that far track.

He learned about hot shots from two days ago when his morning train stopped to let one pass. The conductor had explained to anyone listening how these trains were usually the reason for "Other Train Movement" announcements. That morning's hot shot was in a hurry. This evening's hot shot was not.

The Commuter listened to "Other Train Movement" announcements coming through the speakers over his head as the slow movement of freight cars in front of him seemed endless. The train was headed south, where his train would eventually go when the hot shot got out of the way.

The freight train moved slow enough that the Commuter could read the writing along the sides of the cars using the station's overhead lights. From a few feet away, he read hazardous material warnings on the tanker cars moving past him—liquid petroleum gas, molten sulfur, phosphoric acid, and acrylamide (whatever that was). He got the distinct indication he should not stick around in a derailment.

But he was strong. He could stand against these threats from passing freight cars. After all, the Commuter thought, he rode these rails longer than the careers of most train engineers and conductors. It seemed he had been around for longer than he had lived.

He believed commuting did that to people. They developed a sense that riding the rails caused time to become lost. The Commuter looked up and down the platform at the crowds of people bunched together in places where they hoped the train doors would open. The goal was to get in a car that, when arriving at their station stop, the doors would open close to their vehicles. Being first out of the parking lots meant something to commuters who wanted their commute to end as soon as possible.

Where the Commuter stood, it was further than any of the parking lots. People getting off either wanted to avoid the mad rush or were in no hurry to get home. This meant the mass of humanity was less dense where he stood. Except that didn't help the waiting commuters who were as anxious about the late train as everyone else.

This made the Commuter nervous standing next to the yellow caution strip that marked the edge of the platform. A shift in the crowd and he'd be on the other side of the strip where there was no platform.

Despite these worries, he became aware of a man on his right wiggling his arms like he was trying to shake off bugs, or half-dance to a bebop jazz tune in his head. The Commuter wanted this man to go away. He could make the train even later with his eccentric behavior. People, so worn out from their workday, could start dancing with him or shrieking that there were bugs on that guy.

The Commuter looked around him and almost everyone was reading a book or staring at some video screen. A few seemed to be asleep standing up. No one noticed this stranger that the Commuter turned back to and regarded more closely.

This restless man kept to his own narrow space on the station platform. He stood tall and thin with a long, unshaven face like a sad clown. The Commuter remembered other commutes with this guy when the stranger had dressed in a starched shirt, expensive tie, and pressed suit pants nestled against polished shoes. Today, he wore a brown cardigan sweater too big for him, wrinkled jeans, and sneakers that weren't white anymore. The Commuter got to thinking this man did not have a good day.

He tried not to look anymore at this stranger. Maybe the man would calm down if left alone. The Commuter turned his attention to the slow-moving flats, tankers, and an empty train car with girders sprouting up to hold something that was not there. He wondered if it would rain soon. Cold enough for snow.

The Commuter looked the other way at the far bend in the tracks and away from the guy. The hot shot was not on the tracks his train would be on, so why was his train waiting for this one to go by? Maybe the engineers driving the commuter train knew better than to stop beside freight cars with chemical names.

Down the line, the Commuter watched a boxcar with an open side door coming toward him. It was empty inside. Maybe everything in it fell out, he wondered. He could not help but glance again at the restless man to his right. The guy stared at the empty boxcar coming towards them. His eyes got big, as if he saw the answer to all his problems.

The Commuter wanted to pretend this man was not there. Yet, now a few other people noticed him as he moved his arms and now his feet in more of an improvised jazz beat. Realizing the world was eying him with suspicion, the restless man used his hands to rub his forehead and face like he was trying to hide his head. Except his hands were too small. He dropped his hands and stared again at the empty boxcar.

Commuters were not prone to comment on anything different that might upset their commute. Like this guy with problems in his head. People probably hoped the problem would go away. It did not.

The guy erupted in an explosion of energy, like a rocket launching skyward. He jumped, then took three long steps along the yellow strip, and rushed past the Commuter. In a stumbling manner, he launched off the platform with his arms in the air as if he was trying to fly. The drop of a few feet did not slow him up as he dashed across the tracks toward the open boxcar door.

Everyone in the immediate crowd focused on this guy headed for the boxcar. Except, he stumbled on the first set of steel tracks. Some people turned their faces away, not wanting to see a body cut in half by the heavy wheels of a slow-moving freight car. The Commuter watched the man get back up.

Not hearing the crunch of bones or gush of blood, people turned back to watch the man position himself for a final dash toward the boxcar door. No one said anything as they maneuvered to get a good view.

The Commuter looked around for some would-be-hero to jump down and rescue the guy. No one did. Maybe they were all too surprised, or too cold, or didn't care. In any case, the guy didn't stay still long enough to be rescued.

Good thing he wore tennis shoes instead of his dress shoes, considered the Commuter. The man ran like a gazelle, bouncing up and down until reaching the open boxcar door perfectly. Almost perfectly. Before the watching crowd, the man's foot slipped on the gravel. The crowd gasped, but couldn't look away this time. The man was too close to escaping or dying.

People let out a sigh of relief when he caught his balance, then gasped again as he missed reaching for the boxcar door. He appeared calm and focused as he tried again. This time he held on to the corner of the moving door. One last chance. One good leap. One final grab.

He pulled his torso across the lip of the open door with the ease of Buster Keaton running from the Keystone Cops. Clawing and crawling to get his legs inside, he scrambled all the way in until rolling onto his back. His chest heaved from heavy breathing as he lay there with his arms and legs splayed out, staring at the boxcar ceiling and who knows what. The guy gave a big smile, like he was finally at peace. He was on his way to wherever the freight train was going.

"He made it." Everyone seemed to say this at once. The Commuter realized he had been rooting for the man. He wanted someone to escape this long commute. Someone to find a different way home. The boxcar continued sliding down the steel tracks with the rest of the slow moving, hot shot freight train cars and taking this stranger along.

Commuters in the other clustered groups did not seem to notice the boxcar carrying one of their own away on a different way to commute. They were too immersed in video screens, books, or the back of the person in front of them.

"I took graduate classes with that guy," said a man to the

Commuter's left. It was in this direction that their train should be coming. "We even presented our thesis together a few years ago. He thought his master's degree would get him a promotion. I saw him a few months after the presentation, and he said his company promoted someone else. Someone without a degree. She had special connections, I guess."

The fellow talking had a belly and looked pregnant. The Commuter did not know how the pregnant bellied guy kept from falling forward.

"Yeah, I used to work in the same cubicle farm as that guy," said a second man.

He took the spot on the Commuter's right where the boxcar guy once stood. Everyone filled in the gaps as if it was natural for someone to jump into a moving boxcar and leave an open space in the commuting crowd.

This second man's comb over didn't help his bald scalp from looking blue from the cold. What could be happening to his brain? Hats needed to come back in style, the Commuter wished.

"He was a good worker," said Comb Over. "But he had two teenage daughters and a wife who were always calling him and complaining he didn't make enough money. Maybe it just got to him."

"Women nag and criticize and push you. Sometimes the sex just ain't worth it," said Pregnant Belly on the left.

"I bet he lost his job," said Comb Over on the right. "His company didn't do well in quarterly earnings. I heard that the woman who got promoted over him botched a contract bid. She kept her job, and he probably became the scapegoat."

The Commuter felt like he was in the middle of a ping pong match with these men on either side of him.

"All right. We're going to stop blaming everything on

women," said a woman behind the Commuter. "What we need to do is tell the authorities what this guy did."

The Commuter twisted around long enough to wonder how the grayish woman could talk through the purple scarf wrapped around her neck and face. She punched numbers on her smartphone and each time she hit a button it made a cute little beeping sound. The Commuter watched her long red fingernails cut across her phone, and he could not figure out how she could hit those little buttons so perfectly. He decided not to mess with her. She punched those buttons like she would punch the Commuter if he tried to stop her.

The Commuter looked back at the freight cars slowing down even more. Crap, Purple Scarf was so fast that she caused the hot shot to go to caution. But, wait. That meant my train will be even later, he worried. How did she stop a hot shot freight train with her cute, beeping smartphone? The Commuter wished phones were not that smart. He wondered how the boxcar guy would stay warm. Hell, how was *he* going to stay warm if his train was even later?

"They call it a catch out, what he did," said a man behind the woman.

This man had a gravelly voice like a smoker. This was a non-smoking section, the Commuter wanted to tell him.

"What's a 'catch out'?" Purple Scarf's words could hardly be understood beneath that wool noose.

"It means someone who hops on a freight train."

The Commuter turned around to face this man and wished he hadn't. The woman had stepped aside, and the man had stepped forward into the Commuter's personal space. He had a short gray beard, thin hair on his head swept straight back like he was in a windstorm, and blue eyes. They were the same height, and this man's breath smelled minty that did not mask the cigarette smell.

The Commuter felt compelled to say something. "What's it called when he hops off?"

"Stupid if the train's moving. Arrested if he gets caught. Mostly, getting off, I'd think."

"I guess we won't know either way," said the Commuter. I've got to stop talking to these commuters, he thought. He turned around and looked up the tracks for his train. Overhead, the announcement stated "Other Train Movements" would continue making his train late.

"Well, the emergency dispatcher was going to call someone. I don't know if she'll do anything." Purple Scarf Woman sounded like an annoying buzz.

She started to say something else when the freight cars jumped. Each coupler, where the knuckle joints kept the cars together, let out a sequence of bangs as the line of cars picked up speed. The crowd muttered quiet hoorays. The Commuter noticed another boxcar with an open door and empty insides headed their way.

"Excuse me," said Gravelly Voice in the rear.

He stepped around the Commuter and onto the yellow warning strip. With a single hop, he leaped off the concrete platform, onto the railroad gravel, and toward the boxcar door without hesitation.

Seriously? Another commuter running away? The Commuter watched this guy drop into a sprint, only slower and older that the previous guy, over the empty rails that would one day carry the Commuter's train. The man approached the boxcar door at a steady pace as the train picked up speed.

The Commuter didn't want to look. Yet, he looked along with everyone else as this man took a looping route to intercept the open door. He had long legs, and the Commuter had an open mouth saying nothing.

He wished he didn't have such an excellent view of this man running for the boxcar. The Commuter was still recovering from the excitement of the previous fellow and didn't want to remember amputated or crushed body parts. He needed those memory cells in his head to remind him not to wear the same tie every day.

This second boxcar guy seemed to be better at this than the first guy. He kept time with the train's movement and met the open boxcar door by latching one hand on the edge. In one fluid movement and using the momentum of the fast-moving boxcar, he swung his legs and the rest of his body inside like someone with experience. The train's momentum propelled him into a standing position in the doorway. This guy smiled and waved to the Commuter and the crowd around him as the boxcar took the man away.

"What did you say to him?" Purple Scarf Woman asked.

How can she breathe through that scarf, wondered the Commuter?

"Yeah, what'd he say to you?" Comb Over stared at the Commuter.

"You going for the next boxcar?" asked Pregnant Belly with a smirk.

They're acting like I'm some renegade leader, the Commuter thought. "No, I'm not jumping on a moving boxcar. And, I said nothing to either of those guys."

Great, the Commuter thought. Now people are talking to me. All I wanted to do was stand here quietly until my train arrived and go home. Where's my damn train? He looked down the tracks at the second boxcar guy standing in the opened door yelling at the crowds to get their attention.

People waved, not sure they believed what they were seeing. The second boxcar guy faded into the distance and was gone, leaving the Commuter still waiting for his train in the cold. Is there no end to this freight train? Would the two boxcar guys get off at the same spot and become friends? The Commuter wondered about making friends on the train. He had none.

"I'm going to call again. Someone should know about this," said Purple Scarf.

The Commuter stood there realizing he was not a hero, nor eccentric enough to jump on a boxcar when it's moving. Was that all right, he thought? Yeah, he answered himself. It had to be. After all, what's wrong with being a boring person? I'll just stay here waiting for my train. I'll stand here with these other strangers getting colder. We'll wait together as we do every day. Standing in silence.

The hot shot train picked up speed. Maybe never meaning to slow down again in front of commuters waiting for their late train. One more empty boxcar passed by. No chance anyone could jump on it now. Or at least no one willing to take that much of a risk.

The end of the hot shot rushed past them, meaning their train should be next. The Commuter thought about the home he was commuting to and who lived there with him. A wife who complained he was boring and a daughter who was getting married soon and who seemed to like her future father-in-law more. Neither wife nor daughter ever asked him how his day went.

I don't need an adventure like those two men, he thought. It's the cold I need. It lets me know I'm still alive and not some zombie shuffling back and forth to work five days a week. Although, that's what I'm doing.

As a small boy, the Commuter never imagined he would one day be on a commute where the total miles he traveled felt more than if he had circled the Earth twice. He thought about the two men hanging out in their boxcars. Where were they headed? Freight trains made different stops than commuter trains. He looked at the last boxcar disappearing down the tracks and wondered if it was meant for him to ride on.

The Commuter worried about the opportunities he had to exit his commute. Yet, he forgot all this as he turned with everyone to the toot toot of their train coming around the bend in the tracks. Not too, too late.

Phil Meets Angie

Phil woke up on the commuter train when the back of his neck hurt. He had feared using the tall, round man next to him as a soft pillow and leaned toward the cold train window instead. Unfortunately, this was further than his short neck allowed, giving him the sharp pain in his neck.

Across from the big guy sat a mildly plump woman slouching over an oversized, black handbag in her lap. She was only semi-successful at staying awake and periodically raised her head, rolled her eyes, and dropped back to sleep with a sigh.

Across from Phil, on the other side of the short table, sat a smallish woman dressed in a layer of dark clothes. As she wrote in a blue notebook, her soft lips moved slightly as if she was dictating to herself. Phil watched her head tilt in line with the slant of her pen. Her dark hair looked like black strings dancing on her sloping shoulders.

He looked again at the heavy man who took up a lot of Phil's world in that direction. The bigger the man's features appeared, the smaller Phil felt. Phil worried that the big man might die from a massive heart attack and fall on him. At least the smallish, scribbling woman would record his final moments. Then, maybe someday someone would read how train commuting could be dangerous physically as well as mentally.

Taking a deep breath, Phil decided he wanted a distraction from these thoughts. He dug around in his backpack for his stack of papers that had become the hope of a novel. It was something to work on that would stop him from falling asleep against the window again. As he pulled out the binder of papers, the train jerked to a rolling stop outside a neon lit, concrete platform.

The large man and black bag woman left their train seats to exit the train. Something Phil hoped to do soon. This left him facing the smallish woman who stared back at him.

"Are you writing a book?" She was emphatic, as if there could be no other truth.

"It's a novel about riding this commuter train." Phil was unsure of this woman and who she could be.

"I'm writing a play about the people on this train," she said, with determination and a little confidence.

"Don't put me in your play," said Phil.

"Don't put me in your novel."

Phil decided they were both lying to each other.

"We're both lying to each other," she said. "I'm going to the quiet car to get some writing done."

"I'm Phil. That's the name not to put in your play."

"I'm Angie. Do not put that name in your novel."

She left abruptly, as if she was being chased, although there was no one there. He liked how she said what was on her mind. He wanted to talk with her more, except she headed for the quiet car where he couldn't say anything without being thrown off the train. Phil decided the next time they sat together, he would tell Angie about himself, like most men did.

So, she could properly describe him in her play, of course.

Phil wanted Angie to know about his Japanese mother and Nigerian father and how they never took him to visit either country. However, he'd met a lot of relatives from those countries and felt like he had visited there already. Since I have no siblings to come with me, maybe she will want to visit those countries, he considered.

He planned on not telling Angie about how his ex-wife who crept around with other men when they were married. No, that would not be a healthy conversation, Phil decided.

Phil sat staring at his unfinished novel, wondering how much of his life was in it. He remembered coming home after his first semester at college and finding that his parents had become foster parents. After that, he didn't call them much since he only ended up speaking to one of the foster children. His parents were wonderful with foster children. He wished he had been their foster child.

He wanted to find Angie and tell her these things, regardless of having to be quiet in the quiet car. He packed his papers, but before he could leave, Wanda plopped down next to him with Harry on the other aisle seat across from her.

Phil knew who the husband and wife were because they used their names against each other like swear words. They were continuing a conversation that had obviously started long before they sat near Phil, who wished they had found another seat.

"I won't be home for supper 'cause I gotta make some money when I get off this train," Harry said. He squirmed in his seat as if his butt itched. Or maybe his slim body did not give him enough padding on his butt, Phil hoped.

"What, you robbin' a bank? As if I would've cooked you dinner tonight," Wanda said. "Hey, wait a minute. What did you do with the eighty I gave you this morning?"

Harry wore an expensive looking, dark olive suit, probably silk lined. Any money Harry got probably went immediately out for accessories. Phil looked out the window, pretending the couple was not there. A painful sounding thud made him jump in his seat.

Harry had dumped his hands, palms up, with a thud on the squat table. The guy must be immune to pain, Phil thought, who rubbed his knuckles in sympathy.

"I'm cleaned out, sweetie. Got nothin'," Harry said. "But, it's alright 'cause I'll get somethin' when I get to my 'ppointment." The top button on Harry's pearl white shirt pinched his satin tie close to his neck. Every piece of him looked like a model ready for an expensive shoot.

"I know what you gonna do. You're gonna try and sell that junk car of yours for some ridiculous price. Why don't you just take it to the dump?" Wanda clenched and unclenched her hands in her lap. Her tight jawline left visible evidence she was concentrating on not slapping the crap out of the man seated across from her.

"Baby, you're asking too many questions. I got good business sense. I'm a good salesman."

She threw her arms over her head. "Why am I living with you? You're like a vampire sucking on my affections every night and draining away my money during the day. Your damn attitude and high-priced clothes are out of control." She slapped the edge of the table with both hands, causing Harry to jump back or get his hands slapped.

Phil also jumped at Wanda's violence. Mostly, he worried she had bruised her hands, which would make her angrier. He peered around at the other commuters who pretended Wanda and Harry did not exist.

"I look messy next to you 'cause you're spending all my damn money on making yourself look better than me. Look at this damn spot on my skirt," Wanda shouted.

Of course, Phil looked. She was sitting right next to him and he wouldn't have noticed the spot if she hadn't pointed at it. Somehow, it looked like Harry's face.

"What're you looking at?" Wanda swung her anger at Phil.

"Nothing. Why don't I get up and leave you two here? I think my stop is coming up," said Phil.

Harry said, "Forget that guy. Look at me. I don't know how you stand this commute every day. I'd kill myself if I had to sit here like this all the time. You got a boring life, hon'. Why don't you and I spice it up later? I'll pick you up . . ."

"Spicing it up means sex to you. You know that dump I mentioned? The one where you should take your car? Well, take yourself there instead."

The two sprung into a senseless argument that Phil ignored by staring at his unfinished novel. They lowered their voices, but he still could not concentrate on any writing. Instead, he listened to their argument.

"What's eatin' you? You've got a piss ass little attitude lately," said Harry.

"Shut up! I can survive without your sorry ass. Just watch me." Wanda searched the air above her as if searching for God to help her survive with Harry.

"You can't survive without me just like I can't survive without you. We're stuck together, babe. 'Cept right now I've kinda had it with your uppity attitude. It's nothin' I need," said Harry, thrusting his bottom lip out.

"Good, 'cause I don't need you." Wanda pressed her knees together and clutched her beige pocketbook on top of her little skirt stain.

"What's going on here?" A conductor appeared in the aisle.

"She's a shit ass," said Harry, pointing at his wife's face.

"You, conductor, need an honest opinion. Ask this guy," said Wanda, jutting her thumb at Phil.

"I can't have all of you fighting on this train. You by the window. What's this all about?"

"Why are you asking me? I don't even know these two."

"You were staring at my skirt a moment ago," said Wanda, with a scowl toward Phil.

"You said look at that spot and I couldn't help it," said Phil. He wished he had insisted on leaving them.

"All right, what are all your names?" The conductor pulled out an official-looking pad of paper.

"Harry and Wanda have been arguing since they sat down," said Phil, pointing at the two of them.

"How did you know my name, you nosy ass?" said Wanda.

"I thought you said you didn't know them?" asked the conductor.

"I'm gonna get trashed tonight just so I can forget the both of you," said Harry, standing up and pointing at Wanda, then Phil.

Another conductor arrived.

"Good, go ahead and get outta here, you piece of crap," screamed Wanda at Harry.

"All of you have to get off the train at the next stop," said the second conductor.

The train was already slowing down for the next station when he said this. Phil decided to hold his objections and explanations until they were in the vestibule where the two train cars connected. They would be out of earshot of other passengers and Phil figured he would get one-on-one time with the conductor to explain he really did not know Wanda and Harry.

However, Phil's timing was off. By the time he was ready to say something, he stood with Wanda and Harry on the station platform watching the train leave them behind in a puff of diesel smoke. With the sun setting, the cool air drove down Phil's neck and along his back.

"I can't believe you got us kicked off," Wanda to Harry.

"I'm not responsible for you being a jerk. Now, I'm gonna miss my 'ppointment. What am I gonna do now?"

"Forget it, you two. What am I going to do?" Phil said. He stood on the edge of the platform, past the yellow warning strip, and watched the back of the train become smaller in the darkness. Surely, it will come back to pick me up, he thought. Yet, it continued leaving puffs of diesel fumes behind.

Their train station was next to a swamp that smelled like wet mud. After the train left, so did all semblance of noise, except for movement in the dark trees that Phil hoped were non-carnivorous animals.

"Hey, man. We'll just wait for the next train," Harry said.

"I don't want to wait for the next train. I want to go home," Phil said.

"Home is where the heart is, man," said Harry.

"Shut up, Harry. He don't want to hear your philosophy," Wanda said.

Another argument ensued. Phil moved to the other end of the platform. Half an hour later, the next train came with newer cars and Phil wondered why the newest cars were reserved for the last train that fewer people rode. He also wondered why the conductors kicked them off, knowing they could get on the next train. Sometimes riding the commuter train was not logical.

Phil kept walking toward the front of the train until he found himself in the quiet car, a place Wanda and Harry would never go. Several people were scattered around sitting alone. In an alliance, they looked up, giving Phil their practiced, annoyed expression for making noise by coming in. The self-appointed quiet police, just other commuters wanting authority, were the reason people avoided this car. But at least Phil felt safe from Wanda and Harry.

He did not understand why the train company hooked the quiet car against the train's engine. The machinery powering the train gave off a loud humming vibration that flowed through this car and might have been soothing if it wasn't so annoying. Maybe it was in retaliation against the quiet police.

He leaned his head back against the seat and closed his eyes. The only sounds were the movement of the commuter train from the station and the loud humming sound of the engine. After a few moments of peace, Phil heard the car door slide open. It was not the conductor, but Angie.

She ignored the quiet police and deposited herself in a seat across the aisle and two rows up from Phil. At an angle, he saw her stare at her smartphone with a scrunched-up face. Her black hair, straight nose, and a roundish face made her look younger than him. Or Phil felt older. At the next stop, the quiet police got off leaving Phil and Angie alone.

She did not notice him because he had scooted down with his legs up against the back of the seat before him. It was instinct, the only reason he could explain, to hide from her. What instinct would make him do this? He had no clue. This is my opportunity to talk to her, he thought. He dropped his feet to walk over to her adjacent seat, however, Angie brought out her smartphone at this point.

Thinking no one would hear, she talked about her cancer

and divorce to her mother on the other end. She explained how she got off the previous train and onto this one to avoid her ex. Phil didn't want her thinking he was being sneaky and listening to her conversation, even though he was. So, he kept quiet, wondering what he would do when she finished. Her voice blended with the humming sounds of the engine and he closed his eyes.

He dreamed about a ghost who told him to get a Holstein cow. Phil told the ghost he lived in a one-bedroom apartment near the train station where there was not much room for a Holstein cow. Phil asked if the ghost meant a toy Holstein cow. The ghost apologized and said it meant the suggestion for someone else and disappeared, but not before telling Phil to wake up.

He woke up as the commuter train entered the train yard several miles past the last stop. Angie had fallen asleep, too.

"Hey, we slept past our stop," said Phil, forgetting he was supposed to be hiding from her.

Angie popped her eyes open as if hearing a gunshot. Jumping out of her seat, she ran the wrong way, turned around, and nearly stepped on Phil on her way off the train. A few minutes later, they were standing in front of a small building with a parking lot in front. Nearby sat a van already filled with other commuters who had overslept.

A burly conductor greeted them. "Every evening on every train we have people sleeping past the last stop." He shook his head. "We'd get alarm clocks, but it's not our responsibility to wake you people up."

Phil thought that if the conductors woke people up at the last stop, they wouldn't have to find a ride for them. Also, wouldn't the conductors notice people sleeping on the train as it pulled away from the last station?

"Conductor Cheryl is taking people back to the train station in her van. She has room for one more person. That will be you, ma'am," said the conductor. "We'll have to call you a taxi," he pointed at Phil.

When he got home, Phil decided it was looking like a carry out pizza and red wine night.

Angie's Hope

Angie stood on a concrete platform with navy blue awnings hovering over her head like a shadow. She wanted to be happy while commuting and she arrived early at her train station to stand in front of the crowd instead of behind everyone. Being one of the shortest among her fellow commuters, she knew butts like she knew faces.

Yet, this gave Angie more time to gaze at the train tracks, which mesmerized her in a bad way. With no patience that evening for reading or listening to something, her mind wandered away from her workday and made her remember that this was the anniversary of the operation. A day she wished had not happened.

Two years ago, medical professionals in white smocks and blue pantsuits removed one malignant lump of flesh from Angie's child producing parts. The lump was bigger than they had suspected and, by removing it, they removed any chance she had of having a child. Which she found out in post-op.

When Angie discovered what they did to her, she tried to tell the medical profession they had removed part of her soul and to put it back. She found that white smocks and blue pantsuits are immune to those discussions.

As he drove her home from the hospital, Angie's husband David asked how he was going to have children after she lost what made her a childbearing woman.

"We can adopt," said Angie, although at the time she just wanted to go to bed and stay there. At home, she went in first and stumbled into his packed bags sitting in the foyer.

"I can't deal with your post-cancer. It's changed you and will change you some more. I know these things," said David as sort of an explanation.

"You're a lawyer and know nothing about anyone's cancer. This was my deal and I'm dealing with it okay." Angie didn't dare say how much she was not dealing with it. She wanted to say she wouldn't change, but that wasn't true, either.

"Yeah, you can deal with it, but I don't want to. I'll send the divorce papers."

"Go ahead and leave. You don't need to father any children. You're just like a child," Angie shouted to the mahogany door David closed on his way out. Up to that point, she liked mahogany doors.

That night two years ago, her mother explained through the smartphone, "Now, you're barren. You ain't gonna give me a grandchild."

"This is going to be alright. Just think about it. Without the mess of having a child, I can devote more time to my career and independence."

Angie was sitting at her kitchen table with a small bag of salty chips, wishing the bag was bigger. Her wine glass was ready to be refilled from her bottle of chardonnay. Off to the side, her laptop portrayed an inbox filled with well-wishes from friends and co-workers who knew her enough to know she did not die and was cancer free. They did not know her enough that she wished she had died from the cancer.

"Why did you let them do this to you? What were you thinking?" Her mom's voice sounded like a dentist drill.

Ignoring the glass, Angie took a swallow of wine from the bottle with a few chips before answering. "I had cancer. Don't you understand? Without the operation, I would've died."

"You should have gotten another opinion. You should have talked to me first. Why did you let David make the decision?"

"I was sedated in the operating room and he was there. You didn't want to be there with me."

"I didn't want to be around where they were cutting you up. But it doesn't matter now, anyway. I've got no grandchild coming."

Angie felt like her mother was a bad song on repeat. "I'm relieved I won't have children. I meet mothers all day who will be envious of me."

"You know I'm only looking out for you. I remember how happy I was when I had you and I want you to be just as happy. Why can't you see that?"

"This was not my choice. Sometimes things just happen. Like Dad leaving us for acting gigs in Asia." Angie added that last part to shut her mother up and it worked. Always. Neither wanted to bring up dad's leaving. They had no one but themselves.

Now, two years later and staring at the train tracks, Angie's mother had become as lonely as she was.

The setting sun sent an icy chill down Angie's arms and the back of her legs. She wished she wore a longer skirt or a pantsuit and maybe a heavier jacket. But her smallish stature was easily lost in too many clothes.

The commuter train arrived in a rush, maybe hoping to get this commute over with as fast as possible. Inside the train car,

Angie sat beside a woman who sat tall. This woman leaned her head against the back of the seat without slouching.

Angie became overwhelmed by the woman's skin color, a rich brown that could be chestnut with a little more red. The color exhibited brilliance and passion. Angie grew envious. Her own petite frame was layered in a splotchy paleness like a patchwork quilt.

The woman settled comfortably into an emerald dress overlaid with a floral print that seemed to dance on the green. The woman's short, curly black hair neatly toured her head, accenting her subtle nose, thick lips, and round face.

With a jolt, the commuter train lurched forward. On the voyage to the next train station, the sleeping woman kept sleeping. There was another stop, another station with people getting on and off, and Angie couldn't take the silence anymore. As the train left this station, she asked the woman beside her, "You have children?"

The woman slipped her dark eyes open and peered sideways at her seatmate. "Yes, I have a son. How 'bout you?"

"No, I don't have any children. I'm Angie. You have pictures of him?" Introducing herself always helped ease suspicion of a stranger asking for children's pictures.

Hesitant, the woman said, "I'm Paula. I have some of Jerry on my phone."

Of course you do. What mother wouldn't, Angie thought? From her pocketbook, Paula brought out her phone and swiped through a series of photos. Satisfied with a picture, she showed it to Angie. In it, a small boy with curly dark hair and small palms reached up to catch a big red ball. The boy's wide eyes were frozen in anticipation.

"He's cute trying to catch that ball," said Angie. This was the fourth time that month she had asked a mother about children and got to see pictures. Angie did not believe it was a problem getting a reputation on the train for asking to see pictures.

Paula pulled her phone back and thumbed through more pictures of her son, not caring about Angie. In her pocketbook, Angie's phone vibrated and she knew it was her mother. Angie let it vibrate.

"What does your son want to be when he grows up?" She wanted Paula's attention back.

"Jerry wants to drive a train like this when he grows up," Paula said. "I'd like that. The train is like a straight line home and it's safer than being on the highway. I want my son to be as safe as possible." Paula tapped the top of her smartphone in rhythm to the click clack of the train's wheels as she said this.

"What does your husband do?" Angie asked, dragging Paula's attention back again.

"Sam has a woodworking shop. He keeps pretty busy building furniture. He's also a part-time nurse at the hospital. I like it that he finds time with Jerry, who's his stepson. Jerry's father ran off with another woman long ago. I only ride the train a few times each week. I work from home the rest of the time."

Angie wished she was part of this family. They seemed messed up enough to be normal.

"What about your husband?"

"I'm divorced. I had cancer a few years ago and he didn't want to be around anymore. I think he was just tired of being married." Angie wished she had shut up after the divorce part. She blamed it on the anniversary.

"He sounds like a jerk for leaving you. Maybe you are better off."

"It was two years ago. I'm over it," Angie lied. "It sounds like Sam and Jerry get along well."

Paula crossed her legs to be more comfortable. "Until two years ago, Sam used to play baseball in the county leagues. He hurt his knee sliding into home. Won the game, but lost his knee. It was a bad time for us and he ended up sitting around watching a lot of sports on TV. Bugged the hell out of me."

"Did you take away his TV?" Angie's attempt at a joke made it sound more like a punishment.

"No, I got him to round up some of the neighborhood men and go out to watch the local games and sometimes the high school games. He and his buddies loved the hell out of it. They got deep in the competition. Sam felt like he was playing again. He started bringing Jerry along and the kid loves yelling with his stepdad at all the plays. Now, all the guys bring their kids along."

"I never liked sports that much," said Angie.

"Me neither, but I love watching Sam help Jerry oil a glove or toss a football right before a game. Sometimes they'll shoot a few hoops in our driveway. Sam talks about famous plays he's seen and Jerry listens to everything. Jerry probably can't understand what his stepdad is saying half the time. But he listens. When the men go out with the kids and it's just us women, we get together in the basement of my house drinking chardonnay and getting crazy."

"What do you mean? Do you take off your clothes and run around naked?" Angie tried joking again, having no perception of what "crazy" would be among a group of women. She used to have friends like that, but that was pre-operation and she didn't want to be around them anymore since they all had children. She had no real friends except her mother that didn't count.

Paula stayed quiet for a moment before answering, "Wellll, we certainly have not tried running around the house."

Angie did not know what to say. She looked down the narrow aisle of the train car and saw no one else talking to their fellow passengers. On a crowded train, commuters were often a lonely, quiet group.

"Have you ever been naked in front of other women?" Paula looked out the window as if asking her reflection.

"No, I haven't." Angie tried to make her answer feel as rude as possible. She was not sure whether Paula meant sexually and wanted the conversation to end. She wished she could go in that direction sexually, but men were tragically more attractive to her.

"Don't worry, I'm just trying to get you going. Get you out of that funk you're in. By crazy, I mean us girls shed our emotions and muster as much confidence as we can stand. Some take off their bras, but everyone keeps their panties on."

Angie crossed her legs, but failed to get her skirt over her knees. "What are you trying to tell me? That you're a neighborhood of lesbians?"

"No, we're not into sex. We're into oils. Or at least I am. A few are into watercolor and two work in clay. On canvas or turntables, we remake and recreate ourselves into who we would like to be or who we want the world to see us as. If some of us get topless, it helps us get rid of our inhibitions and improve our creativity. We get into our imagination."

Angie stared at Paula, trying to find the catch to their conversation. "So, you are all artists?"

"Yeah, we have one woman who plays the violin. We decorated a wooden bar stool for her with geometric patterns and brightly colored flowers. She sits on it singing lines of poetry another woman wrote. The musical rhythm keeps us in the creative mood. It gives us hope we can be individuals with families."

Angie tried to understand what she heard. Around her, other passengers moved down the narrow aisle to queue for the next stop. They bumped Angie's elbow as she tried to increase her distance from Paula.

Angie imagined a bunch of topless women in a room smelling of dried clay, leaded oils, and damp watercolors. She pictured coiffured hair, hanging breasts, and wide hips moving about with self-assurance.

Paula continued, "One girl wrote: *Passion creates the want which leads to the love that makes the whole thing complete.* This was part of her poem and I liked how the words sounded. I think of them when Sam is loving me. I think everyone should have some favorite thing to think about when they need some confidence."

Angie sensed her face grow flush and wished she could remember if she ever had that much passion with David. "Who knows about your get together?" She considered getting off at the next stop and waiting for the next train so she would not be tempted to continue the conversation. I might be safe from Paula on another train, but I'd be alone, she thought.

"Everyone knows about us. Like I said, it's not a sexual thing. We're a blue-collar group of neighbors living along a cut-off from the main road next to the train tracks. 'Bout eight houses up our way set off together and secluded by Mackle's creek on two sides, tracks on one side, and the main road on the other. We got 'bout half an acre a piece to pick on and make a garden. We keep busy."

Angie felt like she had no control over the conversation. "You're saying that a bunch of you women go topless and become artists and singers while your husbands and children go off to watch sports somewhere? This is a little hard to believe."

She pictured the houses as a line of identical, Craftsman style design where the homeowners' boredom drove them to look for extremes. I'm not an extreme person, so I won't fit in there, Angie thought. That's what having a dependent mother has taught me.

"You might believe me if you saw some of our paintings. You've ever been in the Oysters and Things? We sell a lot of our stuff there on consignment."

"I bought a painting from there a month ago. It had a woman placing purple flowers into a tall thin vase."

It was the only painting Angie owned. It showed a kneeling woman with her back to the viewer. Possessing a bravely shaved head, the woman curled toward a narrow vase of smoky yellow glass. Three tall, green stems peppered with tiny purples flowed from the glass to kiss a sunny sky-blue canvas. Colors from the flowers echoed onto her long tapered fingers as she stretched to place one more stem into the crowded vase. The woman's perfect human form was imperfect. The imperfect flowers, perfect. The face turned away in shyness.

Angie thought about how the painting captured the smooth contours of the woman's dark skin flowing from her narrow shoulders and over the bony ridges of her exposed spine. Everything ended at widening hips where children could fall out.

"I guess you liked the painting," Paula said.

"Yeah, it was all right. So, did you paint it?" Angie focused on the back of the seat in front of her.

"No, someone else in our group did. However, that naked back is mine." Paula continued her grin. "Two of the women shaved my head for the painting because they figured it'd be more surreal."

"Yeah, it was well painted. But I'm no critic. I buy what I like." Angie thought about the mother in Paula. I could have been reincarnated as Paula's child and things would be processed in a blender instead of a food processor. Angie wondered what a shaved head felt like.

"You've got no children. Why?" Paula asked.

"I don't think that's any of your business."

"Very little is my business. That's why us girls enjoy ourselves when we get together, clothed or not. We're like children talking about our men, kids, dreams, lives, and our dramas. We play together and are not women anymore with responsibilities and regrets. Just a group of girls from dark and olive skin to the blonde hair and blue eye look. I enjoy listening to our twenty-two-year-old newlywed and our eighty-three-year-old grandmother. We're a contrast that writers would crave to know about. So, why don't you have children?"

"I can't. I had that cancer."

"Oh, I'm sorry."

Angie wanted to say something to show she was over it. But she said nothing.

"We don't need to get into this on a commuter train," said Paula. "We'll get into it another time." She paused before continuing, "If you're not seeing anyone, I was going to hook you up with my cousin Joey. He's about your age and a pretty straight guy. He just screws off sometimes, but you could straighten him out."

"I have an MBA. How far did his education go?" Angie felt smug in her answer.

"He's almost finished his doctorate in some engineering area. He just moved here working in the new manufacturing plant outside town. I don't get the importance of gathering these degrees just to prove you're smart enough to do a job."

"It's necessary sometimes. I think it helped me get a job." Angie wanted to add that it gave her self-respect and confidence she did not get from her mother or the people at her job. She noticed the trees outside had disappeared, exposing dark sky as the train crossed a long bridge, high over a wide river.

"I guess owning a piece of paper that says you're book smart can be useful. Wiping your ass with it can be another use, too," Paula said.

"Can't do that, it's too hard. It'll make my ass hurt." Angie scooted down in her seat and kicked up both legs against the back of the seat in front of her in a self-assured position. As an afterthought, she pulled her skirt sharply toward her knees.

"Don't get too comfortable, hon. Last stop coming up," Paula said, grinning.

Embarrassed, Angie sat up, pulled her bag from the floor, and stood. Yet, the train had not fully stopped and the sudden braking action threw her off balance. She plopped down into her seat. Irritated, she pulled herself back up, avoiding Paula's critical eyes, and queued with other commuters.

When the train stopped, Angie stepped down the narrow metal stairs, hoping to lose her co-passenger. Her short legs prevented her from accelerating away. The faster she walked, the more viciously she swung her arms and the slower she felt she was going. With longer legs, Paula easily passed Angie and collided into the outstretched arms of her husband and son.

"I'll bet you two have been to the batting cage," Paula said to her family as Angie walked past.

"Jerry's got to get in shape for the league tryouts in a month," said Sam.

Angie kept walking. As she got to the station stairs, the locomotive let out a loud rumble and towed the cars away. To Angie's dismay, Paula followed her up the concrete stairs toward the parking lot. Overhead, high strong lamps kept the dark away.

Paula caught up and asked, "What are you doing later tonight? There's some game at the high school, so my house is free for us girls. Don't worry. We keep our clothes on for first timers. Besides, it's Friday and you can sleep in tomorrow."

Angie's phone vibrated again. It could be her mother or the child she would have had if she knew how to keep her body from attacking itself. Paula waited a few moments before going back to her family. Angie saw her future filled with ghosts and regrets.

"I'm a writer," Angie called to Paula's back. "At least, I hope to be a writer."

Paula stopped and walked back to give Angie a piece of torn paper with an address and phone number on it. "We don't have any writers in our group. You've got a story to write, Angie."

Sitting in her car waiting for the crowd of vehicles to leave the parking lot, Angie had hope. She memorized the address that could save her. A new world she would visit that night.

She looked across the lot and saw a middle-aged man lean against his car reading a thin book. He looked puzzled over what he read and she watched him thumb quickly through several pages, stop to read a page, and then flip through more pages to another part of the book that did not keep his attention, either.

Tony Breathes

After getting off the evening train, Tony leaned against the hood of his car, watching the rush of commuters leave for the surrounding byways. While waiting, he thumbed through the pages of an old math book he bought at a used bookstore.

It was late September and he was taking his first college class in almost thirty years. He hoped the book's simpler equations would help him remember how X could equal Y. Instead, he found a mystery among the stiff pages.

He tried not to think about the mystery right then. He worried his ego would prevent him from hiring a tutor, meaning he could fail the class. Math had been his favorite subject in college thirty years ago. Somehow that became a long time ago. Now, he tried to understand why he wanted to go back to college at all.

His daughter Carolyn said he was using the class as an escape from what happened a year ago when his wife, her mom, died of a heart attack. He didn't like it when his daughter was right. It made him feel like the child. He closed the book and sighed, wondering what surprises his pregnant daughter would have for him when he got home.

Tony remembered two months ago when she first told

him about changes coming in her life. Changes that included him. He was riding the train home that July day while listening to his daughter's voice, which sounded a lot like her mother.

"I'm telling you straight out, Dad. I'm coming home from college because me and Bobby are having a baby. I know this isn't what you wanted to hear, but it's what I want and it's what'll make me happy. This is so new to me and Bobby. I'm so excited. I can't believe it's really happening—me having a baby. Don't you think it's exciting?"

"You were taking summer classes so you could graduate with Bobby next May. What about *your* college degree?" Tony envisioned his daughter's dreams in diapers.

"There will be time for that later after Bobby graduates and we get married." Through the phone, Carolyn's voice did not sound that sure.

"When will you be coming home?" Tony knew everyone on the crowded train car could hear their conversation. He wished he had Maxwell Smart's Cone of Silence.

"Day after tomorrow. I've cleaned out my course schedule and refunded my books. Some of the courses were not refundable, but that doesn't matter. Listen, I know this wasn't planned, but I'll go back to college one day, I promise."

Tony's hand hurt from clenching the smartphone too tightly. He thought about the quickness of his wife's heart attack that left him facing too many challenges alone. He wondered how much of her death had prompted Carolyn toward Bobby and a baby.

"I'll have your room fixed up and cleaned. I've kept that set of dolls you got when you were ten."

"I didn't know you still had them. They could be worth money."

"Don't worry about money. We'll be fine." He saw no need to save for retirement without his wife to share old age with.

"Bobby will get a job right after he graduates. Then we'll find our own place."

The tall, heavy guy in the adjacent seat glanced at Tony, gave him a weak, sad smile, and went to sleep.

Two days later, Carolyn came home wearing a loose pink blouse hanging over her unbuttoned jeans.

"How long have you been pregnant?" Tony shouted at his daughter's round belly. "You never mentioned you were this far along."

"Bobby didn't want to tell anyone until we were sure. He also didn't want anyone at school to know, either. When I started to show, he thought I should come home in case someone noticed. It's hard to believe I'm only three months and showing this much. Was Mom this big with me?"

Carolyn didn't wait for an answer, which was good since Tony had none. He pulled colorful bright satchels and brown paper bags from the car's trunk and followed his pregnant daughter into the house.

In the months after her arrival and leading up to his present dilemma with the math class, Tony hesitated before entering the house. He dreaded the unexpected changes his daughter might have made that day. So far after coming home, she had draped fabric over the windows in some fashion that made the pattern difficult to look at, arranged the kitchen dishes where he did not normally keep them, and pushed the furniture around in a way that made stumbling into them easy. At least the train schedule stayed reliable for a change.

When the parking lot cleared, Tony drove home where Carolyn met him in the foyer.

"I sold my car. Me and Bobby can use the money to help you out some. I don't want to freeload," Carolyn was enthusiastic as she spun around and led the way into the kitchen.

"You didn't have to sell your car. I've got enough money and daughters don't freeload on fathers. Besides, you'll need something to drive something after the baby is born." Tony followed his daughter.

"Bobby and I can get a car when he graduates. I don't need one when I'm home. I didn't get much for it, but that doesn't matter. It's progress."

He sat at the kitchen table looking at the swirls of reddened pasta. "I guess we need to get the room ready for the baby soon."

"That's what I've been doing all day. I called some of my friends and they're rounding up a lot of baby things. Some of them have kids already. I'll probably need to borrow the car on Saturday. One of my girlfriends wants me at her house. I think they're giving me a baby shower."

"Sure."

"Do you think my baby will have dark olive skin and black hair like your Italian side or mom's side of the family with the Polish and Swedish?" Carolyn asked with a tomatoey noodle lying where she dropped it on her wide stomach.

"You've got both sides of the family — dark complexion, blue eyes, and blond hair. I think your baby will have all of these." Tony noticed Carolyn had not consider Bobby's English-Germanic heritage.

That evening she took the car to meet her friends for "some social time." Tony went to bed early. He worried what he would do after the baby was born. He wondered after the baby became an adult if he/she would ride the same commuter train he did and sit in the same seat he sat in? Tony hoped not. He also hoped he would one day stop commuting.

Lying in bed, Tony thought about the mystery in the math book. It was something else to wonder about other than the approaching birth. He turned his bed lamp on and got the math book out.

The mystery was a postcard dated May 1969 and began on the backside, "Drink cheap wine and dream the dreams." The mystery ended on the front side, showing a passenger train crossing a long bridge over a placid river. Across the bridge's high arches was written, "When I die, I'll come back as a ghost to hide an emerald ring on a passenger train. Whoever finds it will become a hero."

Of course, Tony considered it nonsense that a ghost from 1969 could hide an emerald ring on a train over fifty years in the future. But Tony wanted to believe it could happen. After all, he believed in ghosts and maybe they could do things like this.

The next day, he dropped the math class. The teacher hated teaching, anyway, and was determined to fail everyone. This was Tony's excuse. He thought he could put his energies toward finding the missing emerald ring instead.

That Saturday, he went to the downtown library to read microfiche files from 1969. He figured he'd start there since that was the date on the postcard. Soon, Tony found a newspaper article about a sixty-year-old man who died on the train tracks. A passenger train had hit him without the article explaining why he was on the tracks to be hit. The article also did not explain where on the tracks the man died. However, the article quoted a note found in his pocket that said, "I'll come back to whoever believes in ghosts and show them where to find an emerald ring."

Tony figured it was an emerald ring because that was May's

birthstone, the month when the man died. Did the guy know he would die when he wrote the postcard? Why was it in a math book? Tony decided there were too many questions and maybe when he found the emerald ring he would find the answer to some of them. If he found the ring that probably didn't exist.

The emerald had to be small to be hidden and couldn't be worth enough for him not to commute anymore, unless it came with diamonds. Tony liked sapphires more. If he found the ring, he would add blue sapphires to it.

Since the sixty-year-old died along the same train route Tony took every day to work, he spent his train time looking for the ring rather than sleeping. At least he would not sleep past his stop again. Each evening for the next few weeks, he picked a different train car to ride in. He would have tried looking on the morning trains, but he was not a morning person and slept most of the way.

Tony looked under the seats, in the overhead racks, and along the window edges for some sign of the ring. He tried to do this discreetly so no one would notice. And most commuters didn't notice or didn't care as long as the train kept to its schedule.

Of course, he didn't think he'd find the ring. Secretly, his plan all along was to have the ghost see him looking for it. However, Tony found ghosts could be elusive, even if you believed in them and their silly rings.

After two weeks, Tony lost track of what train car he looked on. Mostly because train cars were switched around a lot. Maybe I should organize a séance and ask the ghost, he considered. Tony wondered if he should focus on something more realistic. Except he had questions. For instance, why the newspaper from 1969 did not print the man's name and why did the postcard have no address.

One evening, Tony asked Carolyn for help.

"I don't know who he was," Tony explained to his pregnant daughter.

They sat at the kitchen table eating chicken noodle soup Carolyn made. Except the chicken was turkey breast and the noodles were spaghetti. Tony stared at his daughter's moving belly. Already the baby was clamoring to get out. He hoped she/he did not take after Bobby.

"Why don't you look up obituaries?" Carolyn asked between spoonfuls of soup she spilled on her chin.

Tony did not tell his daughter how he refused to read obits since he had to list his wife, her mom, in one. "I was hoping the ghost would help me find the ring."

"There's something wrong about chasing after a ring that couldn't have existed. Besides being crazy, it's like you're trying to find a reason to change your destiny."

"Does anyone really know their destiny? Right now mine is you and the baby." Tony did not believe that chasing a ghost could alter his future. Only his dead wife could do that, he decided. He ate a spoonful of watery turkey to keep from trying to explain this to his daughter. He wasn't sure he understood it himself.

"The whole thing sounds suspicious. Anyone hiding things and keeping secrets is up to no good. If someone has to keep secrets, then they are usually doing things that aren't right."

They finished eating and Tony cleaned up the kitchen. He could not think of any secrets he would keep from his daughter. But the dead man had secrets such as where he hid the emerald ring and, more importantly, why? Maybe this proved that secrets lead to obsessions and maybe they were the same,

Tony thought. He obsessed over these thoughts until he went to bed and dreamed about equations. In the dream, math symbols kept him from getting to the train on time.

The next evening, the train stopped on a long bridge with concrete arches rising high over a placid river. Outside his train window, Tony looked down at an unopened green wine bottle. It sat on a breakout ledge wide enough for one person to stand on and get off the tracks if a train came. He wondered if that was the emerald ring. Mostly, he wondered why anyone would walk on the bridge and risk a train coming and needing a place to step off the tracks to avoid it.

After a few minutes, his commuter train crawled toward the next station without being in any hurry. Tony was the last to queue and get off.

"I thought I saw that green ghost you were looking for," said Cheryl, one of the conductors. Tony stopped detraining so she could continue. "There was a flash of green on the bridge we went over. It was brief, but definite. The flash of green."

"Thanks for telling me."

"I'll keep looking."

Tony wondered why. He only mentioned it to a few people who were curious about what he was looking for. Apparently, he wasn't as invisible on the train as he believed.

The holidays came with Carolyn more cautious of who she was becoming in her final trimester. College friends forgot her or she forgot them. She was better at socializing with her high school friends since they knew each other better and most had children.

Carolyn invited her friends and friends of her friends for Thanksgiving that the Piggly Wiggly grocery store catered. It was like Carolyn's last hurrah before being a mother. Many of her friends were already mothers. Tony wondered how many more would be mothers the next year.

Bobby stayed away with excuses of visiting relatives in Europe. Tony thought that was convenient since Carolyn's doctor had suggested she not fly in her final trimester. Some doctors were more cautious than others. He saw his daughter pretending not to care as she enveloped herself in a sea of people from her childhood.

Carolyn repeated the Thanksgiving experience at Christmas. Bobby repeated his European excuses. Tony tolerated the same people again knowing that next year a baby would replace some of her daughter's friends. The house would be a lot less crowded and he a lot less confused about who was who.

In early January, the baby decided it was time to see the world. Bobby came in time to miss the birth by several hours. He entered the hospital room complaining that the baby came at a busy time for him with papers to write. School society dominated his comments as he held his daughter one time, briefly.

"Since you couldn't come up with a name, I named her Alice. Do you like it?" Carolyn looked at Bobby, who looked at his smartphone.

"Yeah, whatever you say." He looked up from his phone. "My parents are coming tomorrow."

Tony thought it sounded like a threat.

Bobby's parents stayed at one of the most expensive hotels and met Tony in the hospital lobby. They explained to Tony what was good for their son. Tony said nothing, for Carolyn's sake, when they said the pregnancy should not change their son's life. It certainly changed Carolyn and him.

"Something should have been worked out," they both explained right before they saw Carolyn for eight minutes and Alice for four.

They left the hospital, taking Bobby with them. Tony wanted to talk to his daughter about the family she was marrying into, but she fell asleep exhausted from this family's visit. He went home to walk into each room looking for his wife's smell.

He always remembered it surfacing in the oddest of places of the house, as if her ghost lingered where it was hard to find. Tony wanted to find the smell and ask her what he should do about the baby and everything. "You're better at this than I am," he told the stale air.

He stopped looking for the smell. It was as elusive as the emerald ring ghost. The next morning when it was time for Carolyn and Alice to be discharged, Bobby did not answer his text or phone.

When they got home, Carolyn sat everywhere holding Alice with baby stuff littering almost every surface of the small house. It wasn't until late afternoon that Bobby and his parents came without excuses for their lateness. All three sat at the kitchen table where Carolyn and Alice spent the least amount of time.

Tony's score for holding Alice that evening: Bobby's parents zero, Bobby once after Carolyn put the baby in his arms (it lasted almost a minute), and Tony who lost count of how many times he held his granddaughter.

It was Carolyn's cooing tenderness toward Alice that kept tense words at a distance. Yet like galloping wild horses approaching, Tony struggled with his anger towards Bobby's parents and mostly Bobby. After two hours and too much talk about wealth, society standing, and the importance of college for Bobby, the three left. Bobby to school and his parents to their luxury house on a lake somewhere. At the goodbye, the only touching was a brief hug caused by Carolyn onto Bobby. Tony held Alice at a safe distance from Bobby's parents.

Tony stayed home for a week to help Carolyn, which included not talking about Bobby. On Alice's one week birthday, he and Carolyn celebrated with a spaghetti dinner. It was interrupted multiple times by Alice's crying, eating, peeing, and pooping. They took turns.

The next week, Tony had to protect what vacation time he had left in case Alice needed him. He found his way back to work. On Wednesday, he came home to find Alice asleep in her rocker and Carolyn rearranging the living room furniture. His daughter struggled with an old, oversized armchair, trying to put it too close to the couch.

"Your mother upholstered that chair and I want it where it can be noticed," Tony said.

"This is a small living room and it will be noticed anywhere it's put," said Carolyn. "Besides, Mom did a lot of things around here and she's gone. I've got a family to worry about now."

"You're too much like your mother, moving away from the past because it's not needed anymore."

"Moving furniture around is not moving away from the past. It's moving old furniture. Here, help me move the couch some more. It's always been in that same place, even when Mom was living," Carolyn grabbed one end of the couch, waiting for her dad to lift the other end.

"Do you have to be so independent about everything?" He lifted the other end.

"I've been messing around with this furniture and knick

knacks all day and I don't like being around so much memorabilia. Bobby, Alice, and I will have our own memories one day."

"I hoped you would want some of these things for yourself."

Carolyn thrust the couch upward a few inches before dropping it with a thud two steps away. "There, the couch can stay there. I can't move it any further. You can put the chair back where it was."

"Wait, help me move the chair back."

"I can't. I can't do any of this. Moving this furniture makes me think about Mom and how she died so young. I don't want Alice to lose me. I want to be there when she has children. Suppose I die and I'm not there to help take care of my baby?"

Tony wanted to say he would be there, but he could only hope he was. He shoved the chair a few inches and thumped it down without looking at Carolyn. Alice was awake by now with all the thumping.

She made noises with her mouth, nose, bottom, or all three. Carolyn took care of her daughter's needs as Tony put the furniture back. When Carolyn returned, they both sat on the couch with Alice between them.

"You and Mom were always a team," said Carolyn, changing Alice's diaper again.

"Now, we're a team," said Tony.

When Carolyn finished, she let Tony take Alice. Carolyn put her head against a short pillow on the couch and soon mother and daughter were asleep. Carolyn with her feet snuggled against Tony's side for warmth and Alice cradled in his arms. Tony sat there staying awake and looking around the room. He spied his math book with the postcard sticking out of the pages. The book and card were too far to reach. Instead, he stayed awake thinking of places on the train where the emerald ring could be hidden.

After a few minutes, Tony got the remote and turned the TV on. He hoped to cut everyone's nap short with the noise since it was almost bedtime. They would end up staying awake past his bedtime and keeping him awake or waking up too early and waking him up. Either way, it would cause his sleep deficit for the week to peak a day early.

Tony watched a program on sterilization. During the vasectomy, a faceless, masked doctor snipped each vas deferens unceremoniously. During a tubal, a woman's fallopian tubes were clamped in a dry medical fashion. Tony changed channels.

Another show had two people building a house for their soon-to-be family. The woman's pink blouse hung over her protruding stomach as she explained the complicated tile pattern that would be her kitchen floor. Tony thought he would get dizzy in the morning if he looked for coffee and saw swirling lines at his feet.

These programs made Tony think about pregnancies, wanted and unwanted. Looking at Alice in his arms and Carolyn sleeping, he saw the semblance of a family. He wondered what would change if he found the emerald ring.

No one woke up, so Tony put Alice in her crib still asleep. He covered Carolyn with a blanket on the couch. In the very early morning hours, Alice and Carolyn were awake, so Tony got ready for the train too early.

The next morning and suffering badly from sleep deprivation, he woke half an hour early worried he would oversleep. He went into Alice's bedroom. Carolyn was enjoying her snoring and Tony could not understand how Alice could sleep with all that noise. He hoped she would not grow up wanting a companion who snored.

Tony picked Alice up even though she had not cried out for him. She continued to sleep. Since he had her up, Tony sat in the room's rocker and whispered details about his treasure hunt to her.

"On the commuter train yesterday evening, I saw a woman who looked like your grandmother. She wore an emerald ring with sapphires. I don't know why she wore something looking that expensive on the commuter train. I asked the conductor Cheryl, who said the woman's ring was an imitation, and she wore it for a class she was taking. Her name was Betty. I think Cheryl was going to introduce us, but my stop came."

Tony wondered what class would require an imitation ring like that. He'd have to ask Betty one day. He stopped talking and wondered how that meant anything with finding the emerald ring and maybe the 1969 ghost.

Alice's small face and tiny head rested in the thick crook of his thin forearm as Carolyn kept on snoring quietly. When it was time for him to go to the train station, Tony put Alice back in the crib and rolled Carolyn over so she would stop snoring.

When he got home that evening, Carolyn met him in the doorway holding Alice. Her face was red and her eyes swollen. She had not heard from Alice's father in two days.

"I tried texting him and he never responded. So, I called him over and over until he answered the phone. He said his parents told him Alice was not his child."

Carolyn held up the palm of her free hand towards her dad's face. "Before you say it, I don't want any testing done. Decisions have been made. It is his loss and not mine."

"I want to help you get through this," Tony said to Carolyn.

"We are getting through this," Carolyn said as Alice burped in her arms. This was followed with a chorus of spittle and a string of formula that the baby let flow out of her mouth like vomit was another form of language.

Carolyn cleaned her daughter, sat down on the couch, and turned on the TV to watch an old western sitcom. Tony was glad not to have any more conversation about the Bobby matter. He was upset enough and talking about it would make him more upset. He needed time to process things and sitting together quietly did that.

Half an hour later, Tony went into the kitchen and brought back a bologna and cheese sandwich and Cheerwine soda for Carolyn and himself. He brought a bottle for Alice since she had discharged what was in her stomach. Father and daughter sat on the couch sharing a bag of chips and watching the western sitcom marathon until it was time for early bed.

"Thanks for not wanting to talk about Bobby. I need some quiet time to process it all. But this is a warning. We're talking about him tomorrow when you get home," said Carolyn with a smile and a hug with her dad.

"I'll be ready," said Tony. He thought they already talked a lot just sitting together.

The next evening, his daughter had already talked about Bobby to her friends. All that was left were summaries of her conversations. Tony reluctantly accepted the summaries. Any details, he would need to ask her friends.

The next day, Tony took the noon train and stopped by an animal shelter on his way home. No, he did not know what he was doing. He just thought they all needed a pet.

The beagle smelled Tony first. Unknown to Tony, but noticed by his fellow workers, he had a sweaty, sour tinge to his skin that made the beagle howl loudly. Tony walked over and brought his face close to the dog's wire cage. The beagle sprung out with a quick lick through the wire mesh. She seemed to smile, which felt good to Tony.

On the way home, Tony called out "Mary" for a name. The beagle barked with enthusiasm. She had no clue what Tony said. The name just sounded like small bells.

"Don't bark when we go in. Alice may be asleep," Tony said.

He opened the door and Mary dashed into the living room, letting out a howl that echoed deep into the house. Communication was always important to Mary.

"Why did you bring home a dog? There's enough to do taking care of Alice," Carolyn said. She held Alice up so the jumping beagle would not lick the baby's feet.

"I thought a dog would round out our family. Also, Alice needs to grow up with a pet."

"You got this dog to replace Bobby, didn't you?" With her free hand, Carolyn tried to push the dog away. The dog slobbered her hand with a big lick.

"Maybe, yeah. But that dog will be a better companion than Bobby and his stupid parents." Tony tried to put a lease on the beagle's collar to get her away from Carolyn, but he ended up chasing the dog in circles around the living room. The furniture got in the way, catching her.

"You're at work all day. I'll be the one taking care of it." Carolyn watched the dog let her dad get near before darting away in the other direction.

"This beagle is going to love and appreciate you for it. You think Bobby would have done the same?"

Tony stopped chasing the dog since he was out of breath. He faced his daughter as the beagle danced around, wanting to play more.

"You're going to have to name this dog. I already had to name Alice," said Carolyn.

"I already named her Mary."

"You what?" Carolyn looked at her dad with an opened mouth. "What were you thinking? Did you forget that Mom's name was Mary? That your wife's name was Mary? What are you trying to say here? You think your wife was reincarnated as this dog? You think this dog can take the place of my mom and your wife?" The questions flowed out of Carolyn's mouth like blood from a cut artery.

"The dog liked the name."

"How many names did you try on her? One?"

Mary let out a howl and dashed into the kitchen. Carolyn handed Alice to her dad and stomped after the dog that kept howling.

"What do you want?"

Mary thought it obvious since they were in the kitchen with lots of food smells. She made it simple by thrusting her nose toward the pantry where she smelled potato chips.

"She's hungry," Carolyn said, who filled a bowl with pellets from the bag of dog food her dad brought home.

Mary put her nose up close to the bowl to make sure all the space was occupied with pellets. She got close enough that some fell on her nose and dribbled to the side of the bowl. As Carolyn put away the bag, Mary flipped some hard pellets behind the food bowl for safekeeping. This was just in case these people forgot her, since she was a new experience for them.

Before Carolyn could leave the kitchen, Mary went to the back door and scratched it with her paw. She knew doors meant outside, and she wanted to see if it was grass or concrete. As Carolyn took Mary outside for a pee and poop, Tony changed Alice's pee and poop filled diaper.

Outside in the chilly air and in the grass, Mary thought this was a good family to love and who would love her in return. Despite their arguing.

"This dog will stay locked in the house most of the time. You're trading one prison for another," Carolyn said, meeting her dad in the kitchen.

"Our home is not a prison." Tony thought about his office cubicle and how it could be called a prison. "We can all walk her in the evening when I get home. Like a family."

"We don't know where this dog came from."

"She came from the animal shelter. When you brought Alice home, she came from the hospital. The shelter is just another hospital. The dog had all her shots, was cleaned, had her nails clipped, and teeth brushed. She's better taken care of than me after riding the crowded commuter train."

"I hope it's been spayed or neutered or whatever they do to make them not attract other dogs," said Carolyn. "We don't want any unwanted pregnancies."

The evening became a flurry of adjustments to make sure Mary's cage was in Tony's room. At bedtime and moments after shutting the cage door, Mary started howling. Apparently, she had enough of sleeping alone in the shelter. Tony didn't like the cage, anyway. At least Mary didn't snore as she stretched out across the middle of his twin bed.

That night, Tony dreamed the 1969 ghost was telling him about destiny. Tony did not want a ghost talking about his destiny, no matter what year it came from. He wanted the ghost to explain what the emerald ring was about. Only Mary could tell him about destiny. His wife, not the dog.

Tony woke up an hour before the alarm with Mary pushing her paws into him to get more room. He rolled over to face her and got a wet lick in the face.

"It is not time for me to get up," said Tony, worried about his mental state for talking to a dog while losing sleep.

Mary rolled over on her back and Tony scratched her belly, thinking about destiny. "Nothing ever happened to me until Carolyn was born. I spent as much time as I could with her, but I had a long commute on the train. I resented the train ride because it took me away from Mary and Carolyn. Yet, I kept commuting because of the retirement package. I figured if I held on until I retired, there would be plenty of time to spend with them later. Now Mary is gone and Carolyn is grown up."

He turned around and looked out his window at the lights from other suburban houses, switching on like miniature suns pushing away the night. Tony assumed other commuters were starting their daily journey like he should do. He turned back to Mary who stayed on her back waiting for more belly scratching. Tony got up to take a shower. Mary went back to sleep satisfied with the belly scratching she received.

In the kitchen, Carolyn was already hassled trying to get Alice ready for her first pediatric checkup. Mary howled until Tony called work and took the day off. On the way home from the checkup, the weather was warm with sunny skies and they stopped at a park with swings. Tony and Carolyn took turns swinging their legs in the air. Alice smiled a lot watching them.

Mid-February entered with a blowing snow that imprisoned everyone inside the house. Tony cleared a wide patch of snow for Mary to pee and poop outside. Except, the snowbank was much more fun and Mary came out of it each time with ice balls dangling from her fur. Carolyn cleaned off Mary so she did not to leave wet spots on the kitchen floor. Her dad came in dripping with melting water. Mary gave Carolyn a surprise lick for not complaining.

That afternoon after the sun warmed the air enough, Carolyn came out with Alice bundled up so much she looked like a snowball. Mary covered herself in ice balls again. That night, with Mary already in her favorite spot on the bed, Tony realized he was thinking less of his wife's smell.

On Saint Patrick's Day, Tony looked again on the train for the emerald ring. At work he used the old math book to calculate the distance across the train bridge, where he saw the green wine bottle. He found that by a factor of ten, plus or minus a factor of infinity, the distance was equal to that between where he lived and where he worked. Would he walk across a train bridge where the wine bottle sat to see if there was something inside like a ring? Thirty years before he may have tried.

On Friday evening, Tony watched for the wine bottle on the train bridge. The train went fast, but it was there on the ledge, unmoved by the train's speed. When he got home and before taking off his coat, he kneeled down so Mary could get some good licks in on his chin. The rich smell of Carolyn's Italian cooking bathed the house in warmth, even if the food tasted like Spain.

"Treasure hunts are only good if they end up with a treasure," Tony told Carolyn that evening after supper. Their dessert was a small dish of chocolate ice cream with a slice of mozzarella mixed in.

"Chasing after that dead man's ring is making you look foolish. You know that ring can't possibly exist." Carolyn ate her ice cream with olive oil drizzled on top.

"You're right. Besides, if there was a ring it would just be a green rock with metal around it. A few days ago, Cheryl told me she found more about the emerald ring man in some old train files. The man rode a passenger train and got off at the station across from the bridge where he bought a bottle of wine. He walked back across the bridge to that ledge and put the wine bottle there. He was walking back across the bridge when the train hit him. The note was found in his pocket. So, that's the end of that story."

"Except the green wine bottle is still there," said Carolyn.

"Don't worry, I have no intention of walking across the train bridge to get it," said Tony.

He didn't think wine from a fifty-year-old green bottle would be drinkable. He was more amazed the bottle lasted on the ledge for so long. Maybe the ghost was protecting it. Tony wondered if this was what he was supposed to find.

They ate their ice cream in silence for a few minutes.

"Someone needs to make sure your mother is all right on the other side," Tony spoke quickly. "I think the train ghost is making sure of that as long as I'm looking for his emerald ring."

"I'd like to think Mom is doing just fine and busy watching over us."

Tony looked down at Mary and gave her a treat he had been keeping next to his plate. He looked at his daughter and said, "I wanted to give you the emerald ring when I found it. I wanted you to have a treasure. I thought if I found that emerald ring, we'd be alright."

"Everyone here is my treasure," Carolyn said while cleaning Alice's face. "Love comes from one person paying attention to someone else. The four walls of any house can quickly become a home with a smile from one person, or dog, to another."

"I wished I had spent more time with you and Mary instead of riding the train all the time," said Tony.

"I always liked you riding the train. I always knew where you were. Besides, we had enough adventures on the weekend and your days off," said Carolyn. She finished cleaning Alice, then used the same cloth to wipe Mary's whiskers. Neither seemed to mind.

That night, Tony put the old math book with the postcard at the bottom of his bureau drawer beneath his underwear. He did not need his life derailed by something like a mystery. When he got in bed, Mary licked his ear once and curled against his warm back.

Through the bedroom wall, Tony listened to Carolyn sing a lullaby to Alice. He hoped the child could get the off-key song out of her head. With Mary snuggled next to him and Carolyn's singing, Tony caught a whiff of his wife's smell and knew they would be all right.

Who's Listening?

"Hi! This is Sheila."

Phil woke with a start at a woman's squealing voice. It came from a tallish woman sitting across from him in the train seat and facing him. She held a pink smartphone hard against her long, blondish hair and continued a conversation as if she was the only one on the train.

"This should stay between me and you. So, listen. This is what I was thinking. I don't think her menopause is all her problem. Instead, I think Mom's got the wrong mentality about Dad and his heart issue."

A short plastic table between them held Phil's boring paperback. Since he was now awake, he opened his book and tried to forget he existed in a crowded train car rebreathing other people's breath. He pulled the paperback up to his face, hoping to block Sheila's face and her shrill voice.

"Yeah, that's what I'm saying. Dad's a patient of Mom, and she's a patient of him. They're all nothing but patients and me being like a nursemaid living with them."

Phil dropped the paperback onto the table and watched Sheila sweep her tongue quickly across her pouty lips, lubricating them to shrill out more words.

"That's right! Exactly. Like I was saying. It's that mentality of theirs. Blaming it all on their physical problems. What about my feelings? They need to consider me, too."

I won't continue sitting here listening to this, Phil decided. It was fight or flight and he was too tired to fight. He looked around to move to another seat, but all the train seats had people sitting in them. Several of these commuters looked at Phil and nodded toward the woman, hinting he should do something about her loud talking.

What am I, the quiet police? These were the commuters in the quiet car who self-appointed themselves to maintain the silence by telling people entering the car to be quiet. The quiet police were the most talkative. Phil figured he had enough responsibility aligning his life around train schedules. Besides, he did not have the motivation to confront annoying people like this woman after a week of commuting. He went back to his paperback, so he couldn't focus on with her shrill voice.

"Don't say that! You're the fourth person to say that to me today. I'm not cute enough to find someone. It's like saying I'm a puppy dog, and good enough to be adopted."

Phil's hands gripped the edges of his book as Sheila's voice hit an even higher note. The sound bit into his eardrums like needles. She stretched her free hand out on the table, admiring her nails as if the painted fingernails were the most beautiful thing she had ever seen.

"Whatever. I think you're pretty and your daughter will grow up like you because she takes after you and both of you will always be pretty. I'll never get to that point in my life. All I'll be doing all my miserable life is taking care of sick, old parents because they'll live forever. Although I hope they don't die. I couldn't take that."

A pause before she said, "Whatever."

"Whatever," mumbled Phil.

"Whatever."

"Whatever, whatever, whatever," Phil said a little louder. Apparently, Sheila did not hear him. But a gray-haired woman one seat up did. A gruff looking, tall man one seat over gave Phil a scowl like this was a wimpy approach. Phil decided not to look at them anymore.

"Yeah, you have this perfect life with a perfect baby and husband and I've got nothing."

"Could you lower your voice, please?" Phil asked in his normal tone. He wanted some hope of forgetting her voice before it scarred his brain.

"Okay, so you're not perfect all the time. But listen to this and don't let it go beyond me and you. I know I'm not pretty. I can be a slob sometimes. I should wear better makeup and go to some specialist who specializes in making people look special. You've got a natural, clean, good look. You barely wear lipstick and mascara. I have splotches. I've got a look that needs a lot of work."

"Your loud voice could use a lot of work, too," Phil said in a louder voice.

"Shut up. This is a private conversation. Oh no, not you. It's some guy across from me who's being rude. Go on."

Sheila licked her lips for more lubrication.

"Exactly. Babies are the start of life and menopause starts the end of life. And here I am stuck in the middle, waiting for one and taking care of the other. And then there's Dad. It's like, you know."

"No, I don't know. Why don't you tell me?" Phil thought he could be an extraterrestrial with antennae sticking out of his head and she wouldn't notice.

"It all makes me scared. Mom just doesn't understand

Dad's condition and Dad does not know what Mom is going through. Who knows? Maybe I'm the only one to understand Mom and Dad. But I can't tell them nothing."

"I don't want to understand you or your family," said Phil.

"Whatever. I know you're right. I knew that would happen. I knew you and your husband would fight over that. Then, you two would make up because you have your little girl. She's so right for both of you."

"This train is going to the constellation Pegasus. Next stop is the star Epsilon Pegasi," said Phil. He knew this only because it was in the book he was reading.

"You're an annoying person," Sheila said, pointing at Phil. "No, not you. This guy across from me. But, Sis, I forgot to tell you about my date last weekend. He tried to make me think he was so cute. He was, but that's beside the point. He had such an ego. I don't need that. I need someone strong who'll pay attention to me."

"I'm trying to read," Phil said, pointing at his book.

"I thought you were going to Pegasus. No, not you, this guy. Anyway, there I was at this bar with Mr. Ego. It's just that I wanted him to stand up to me and tell me how he feels. He only noticed me when I blocked his reflection in the bar mirror. I was practically standing on the bar doing this. It was so like him not to notice me."

A conductor hurried past, ignoring Sheila's loudness and not giving Phil a chance to get his attention. He started to go after the conductor, but people began queuing up for the next station and the aisle filled quickly.

"I should have said something to Mr. Ego, but it doesn't matter. I left Ego at the bar and went home. Mom was there checking on Dad. He had that triple bypass and I'm still not sure what that is. If Mom knows, she's too involved in her hot flashes and checking on Dad to explain it to me."

Torn between pushing his way into the queue or saying something to Sheila, Phil sat there staring at his book. He considered leaving it on the table when he got off. It was not good and seemed like a waste to carry it any farther.

"No, I think you're wrong. Mom needs to get over this menopause thing. She and Dad have lived a whole life together and she's always complaining about him. Dad's a sweet man who was always there when he could be."

"Sheila, you want this book?" Phil slid it over to her as a distraction.

"Do you want me to take the book and throw it at you? No, not you. This guy across from me, again. Anyway, I don't regret Dad being at work all the time. He had to support us. Mom was always sick or had something wrong with her. That's what she's doing now. Trying to get sympathy. But I'm not giving it to her."

"Sheila, I don't want to hear about your family problems anymore," Phil said, almost shouting at her.

"Didn't I tell you this is a private phone call? Yeah, the same guy." She paused to take one breath. "Exactly."

Phil wondered why her signal hadn't given out. Technology had gotten too good.

"I thought you were my sister and friend. I don't like you saying things like that. You're pissing me off now. So what if Dad was never around much? So what if he liked his work more than us? His work was important, though I don't know what he did. You should know. Don't you?"

"I'd like to know. Can I talk to your sister?" Phil tried to outmatch Sheila's voice. He wasn't shrill enough.

"Yeah, yeah, whatever. I'll be nicer to Mom. All right, already. I said I'll try. Why don't you come over more and see what's going on and how much I hate everything? This thing that's my life is destroying me right now. I'm living with my parents and I'll be thirty next year."

"We are almost at Epsilon Pegasis. This your stop? If not, why don't you get off, anyway." Phil wished there were more star names in the boring book.

"Shut up. No, not you. Yeah, that guy. Anyway, you got your little girl to take care of and you're good at that. I could be good like that with a baby. Damn it, I'm getting old. Pretty soon, wrinkles will take over. Then everything will start sagging and I won't be able to have children."

Phil got up to go to another train car, except commuters still clogged the aisle. It was a popular stop and commuters queued up too early. He sat down to wait.

"Thanks for saying that, but I don't believe anyone will ever love me. Really. That's what's wrong with you. You're always seeing the bright side of things. I think you need to be in my shoes for a day. See how it feels to be dealing with all of this."

"I and everyone on this train car can hear what you're saying." Phil leaned across the short table and said this loud enough that Sheila couldn't ignore him.

"Well, no one had better be listening to me! This is a private conversation. And no, you can't talk to my sister." She matched Phil's lean until their faces were inches apart.

"I want to read my book," Phil said, tapping his paperback with his index finger.

She held the smartphone five inches from her ear in launch mode. "I want to finish my conversation."

He stared. She stared.

"This guy sitting across from me interrupted me again," Sheila said into her phone while slamming herself back in her seat. "Yeah, I can come by tonight. I'd like that. We can play some board games. You'll have to find games for three people and not four. What? Oh, I don't know. How old are you?" Sheila looked at Phil.

"Thirty-one." Phil spoke before he could think of saying it was none of her business.

"He's two years older than me. Can you believe it? Yeah. What? All right, all right. What's your name?" She faced him again.

"Phil. Now, can you please end your conversation?" Phil was quickly ticked off with himself for obeying her.

"His name's Phil. No, he doesn't have any ring on. Hey, Phil. You committed to anyone?"

"That's none of your business."

"No, he's not committed. Yeah, yeah. Whatever. I'll see you tonight."

Sheila slipped the smartphone into her bulky bag like an old West gunslinger packing her piece.

"Hey, guy," she said, sitting with empty hands stretched across their table. She had red nails and long fingers.

"I'm trying to read."

"Yeah, so I see that, except your book is closed. Also, you tried to give me the book to read, so it can't be that interesting. Hey, you want to play cards? I've got a deck in my purse and we've got an empty table in front of us. Few people on this train's got a table like what we got."

Phil watched Sheila watching him.

"I guess so. This book is boring."

Sheila whipped out a worn deck of cards. Shuffling in front of Phil, she said, "So, what are you doing tonight? You want to be the fourth in a board game?"

The Bathroom on the Train

Riding the evening train home, Clyde stared at the back of the seat in front of him. He worried that his life was half over. At thirty years old and at three hundred pounds, another three hundred pounds in thirty years would certainly kill him. Entering this second part of his life, Clyde wanted to be someone other than a lonely fat man and maybe live a little longer.

He wondered if his ancestors had been this big. He learned that his Jewish side, with the Middle Eastern skin tone, had lived a long time if they avoided being killed by people who hated Jewish people with a Middle Eastern skin tone. Some could have gotten this big. While Clyde got the skin tones, his looks were more like the Romanian side of his family who immigrated from Transylvania.

He wished vampires existed, and he could find one who liked to drink fat rather than blood. Clyde could keep someone like that alive for a very long time. Sitting in his train seat, he let his heavy body shift with the train's motion while remembering his mother. Only because she had just died and the reason he needed to make changes in his life.

He last saw her one month before his thirtieth birthday, which was one month ago. Her body had finally given up on carrying around too much fat as she laid in a hospital bed surrounded by beeping machines. Clyde had no sympathy for her after years of tolerating her self-love, selfish demands, and self-centeredness.

"Your father never loved me, so I made you fat, too. That way no one would love you and it would always be just us," his mother said from her hospital bed.

"I was a fool to love you and should have realized you had no love for me. All you ever cared about was yourself." Clyde stood near the door, prepared to exit forever. He remembered how he did not want their relationship to survive any longer.

"It's your father's fault. He didn't give me enough attention, so I had you. I wanted someone to love only me."

"I don't love you anymore." Clyde wished he could rip his fat off right then and suffocate his mother with it.

"You don't mean that. Help me live. I don't want to die. Save me."

"I'm fat because of you. Who will save me?"

"You'll be fat the rest of your life. I know a secret about you and why you'll never find a woman to love. And that secret will keep you fat."

"I don't believe you. I will not be fat anymore."

Her side of the family planned the funeral he did not attend. On his thirtieth birthday, he celebrated at home with a large pizza and large sweet tea. He loathed his lack of self-control and started a diet the next day.

Over the next few weeks, Clyde tried several diets to change into a person whom someone could love. Except, he hated the restrictions, and the controls demanded of him. The diets reminded him too much of his mother's demand for control.

Earlier that day, before the evening train home, he started a new liquid diet. Clyde figured he had a chance to lose some weight since he considered liquids not as fattening as food. Except, all day he kept leaving his cubicle to go to the bathroom. Each time he went, he peed so hard that the urine splattered off the urinals and onto his pants.

The width of his body prevented him from seeing the wet spots, but he could feel them. He hoped the paper towels he used got most of the dampness off so it wouldn't smell. Fortunately, his body size kept people from getting too close, anyway.

Before getting on the commuter train that evening, Clyde peed one more time in the bathroom across from the train station. He hoped it was good enough until he got home. Yet, after almost an hour later on the train he had to pee again.

He wanted to wait until he got home and use his own bathroom. Thinking about his extra-large bathroom with the extra-wide toilet seat made him want to pee more. Letting out a sigh, Clyde surrendered to his urge and looked down the narrow aisle toward the bathroom at the end of the train car. Pushing his way there meant people would lean away from him as if his fat was contagious. Yet, he could not wait.

When he stood, a flicker of the overhead lights passed through the train car and the constant rush of cooling air spit instead of blowing. Surely, he did not weigh enough to cause electricity to shut off. At least, he hoped not. Just as quickly, all things electrical returned to normal. As if impish gremlins darted between the seats playing hide-and-go-seek with the electricity.

"We're having some power problems, folks. But I think we can keep things running to the end of the trip." Over the loudspeaker, the conductor sounded tired and unconvincing.

Everything electrical continued to be bright and cheerful like it would stay that way, so Clyde went for the bathroom.

The only other choice was to pee in his pants and he had enough pee stains there already. He left a swath of commuters returning to their upright positions.

Going in a place made for skinnier people, Clyde locked the pocket door with the slide of a handle, push of a latch, and pull of a lever. Or something like that. Facing the stainless steel toilet, he aimed and let loose.

He relished the instant relief. In the brightly lit, closet-like room, he felt his swollen bladder slowly deflate. He leaned his head back and closed his eyes to drink in the satisfaction as the heavy weight of his body sagged with the easing of his discomfort.

Clyde felt fat. Fatter than he had ever been. And he did not think the extra liquid he drank was draining away any of this fat. He wondered what secret his mother meant, and he hoped it would not haunt him.

Clyde finished peeing, zipped up while avoiding any flesh, and opened his eyes. All he saw was darkness.

At first he thought he had died or gone blind from peeing so much. Except he heard people on the other side of the bathroom door complaining about there being no electricity. Clyde turned and faced the pocket door as a rising sense of helplessness blocked his memory of what knobs and handles he pulled or pushed to lock himself inside.

He yanked on the metal handle, but of course it didn't move. He fought down a tightening anxiety, realizing he was trapped in a train car bathroom. Taking several deep breaths to calm down, Clyde waited for the lights to come back on so he could see how to get out. He stood in the darkness letting his rolls of fat chase after the train's rocking motion. Surely, the conductors would not let passengers ride in darkness to the end of the trip.

"We apologize folks, but our power will be off for the rest of the trip," the conductor shouted from somewhere in the train car. "That way we'll keep to our schedule."

Clyde fought down the urge to kick the door and beat it with his fists. But he remembered the door being pretty hard. It's all right, he thought trying to calm down. I'll feel around the bathroom until I find all the knobs, levers, and latches. I should have time before the last stop.

"Last stop coming up," said the conductor as his voice faded into the next train car.

How long was I in here? Clyde worried he had slipped into an alternative universe. He had hoped he would be thinner in a world other than his own.

He opened his eyes wider to let in more light, but it did not help. The tiny room had no extra light to let in. All Clyde saw were shadows and he hoped they were not ghosts of former commuters or his mother. With his chubby hands, he fumbled for the door handle hoping to feel his way out.

Carefully, he found a rubber slide and a small latch he slipped out. Thinking he had saved himself, he yanked the handle twice—hard. It made a clanging noise without opening. He yanked again and created the same clanging sound. Somewhere in the darkness of his prison was another locking mechanism. He felt the train slowing down for the last stop.

Again, Clyde jerked hard on the handle and sent another metal clang into the train's hallway. A noise loud enough to tell commuters who might have heard that they had captured a stupid, fat man in the train's bathroom. Desperation grew in him as his bathroom prison stayed dark and might have even gotten a little darker.

The train continued to slow and maybe this was how

things were meant to be, Clyde thought. Everything was normal except that it was pitch black inside a train car bathroom with a sliding pocket door that would not slide. Clyde wasn't even sure he could find the toilet again if he had to pee. This last thought made him anxious about peeing.

Attempting to calm himself down, he closed his eyes tightly and rubbed his hand across his loose, thinning hair. Tension caused sweat to run down the fleshy folds of his back. Clyde felt dizzy and wondered if he was still standing or had fallen on the floor.

Of course I'm not on the floor. There's not enough room for my body there. Clyde felt the train slowing down as he kept his eyes closed to help him concentrate. He clenched the metal handle, partly for balance and partly for hope.

Maybe I peed my soul straight out of my body, he thought. Maybe I died and am safely in the afterlife. Clyde realized that if his afterlife was being stuck in a commuter train bathroom, then he was in hell.

He felt ugly and forgotten; hidden inside this bathroom prison with the fatness of his body. With no real solution, and hearing people queuing outside the bathroom door, Clyde decided he would try one more pull on the handle.

He knew that, with this pull, people would definitely hear his desperation. Later they would spread the joke about the fat man trapped in the train car bathroom. He didn't care, even if he did.

Clyde took a deep breath, tensed his body with what muscle he could locate, and popped open his eyes for the big pull. He had to blink twice from the dim lighting.

The lights were on half power, but enough for him to spy a locking lever off to the right where the pocket door slid into the wall. Lunging for the silver handle, he slammed the lever and his knuckles against the wall. Rubbing his hand, he heard something release. With his chubby fingers holding the door handle, Clyde slid it easily open like everything had all been a practical joke by those fantasy gremlins.

Released from his bathroom prison, Clyde took two steps up the narrow aisle to queue with other commuters. He kept his eyes down, avoiding contact with anyone who might have heard him struggling to open the door. When no one said anything, he looked up.

No one paid him any attention. They were all mesmerized with their electronics or in anticipation of getting off the train as fast as possible in that competitive spirit Clyde sometimes fell into. He grew angry that no one knew about the trauma he just gone through. He did not like that he was a thirty-year-old fat man who no one noticed had been in trouble.

Looking around at his fellow commuters, all familiar faces from years of commuting together, Clyde grew less angry. He realized that the sameness of commuting had created a numbness among everyone, so that no one noticed banging from the bathroom. Like himself, his fellow commuters had become too familiar with the commute.

Clyde was still angry he went unnoticed. Suppose I had died in there? He worried about his life already shortened by being fat and alone and he did not see any sense to this stressful travel except to shorten his life further. Like his weight belonged to him, Clyde feared he had become the commute.

I don't want my fatness and I don't want to continue commuting, he thought. I want something else — freedom from the first thirty years of my life. A different direction and happiness. Clyde struggled with his thoughts as the train stopped and the exit doors slid open. He did not move. He couldn't. He wasn't sure if it was anger or fright that made him stand there unsure about what to do.

If I go to my apartment, there will be eating. If I go out, I only know places that smell of grease with cooks standing in front of long hot grills. None of these places had chefs. People behind Clyde urged him to move out of the way. They pushed his fat around to get past. He shoved his bulk into the bathroom and slid the door shut to get away from them.

He didn't lock it this time in case the electricity went out again. On the other side of the door, Clyde listened to the last of the commuters tromp off and for long minutes the train did not move when it should. Eventually he heard a person approach.

Someone must have told the conductor that a fat man was hiding in the bathroom. The conductor did not try to open the door, but knocked three times.

"You alright in there?" she asked.

Clyde slid open the door and tried not to look at the tallish woman sporting a blue hat with a gold emblem on the front. Her name tag said "Cheryl."

"My mother did this to me," Clyde said. "She died and left me with no one to talk to about what to do next."

Cheryl hesitated a moment, and started to say something, but Clyde was not sure if it would be to him or to the speaker box on her shoulder. He did not want to risk having more people show up asking him if he was all right. He used his size to leave her behind. Walking off the train, Clyde was glad there was no crowd to greet him and see what had happened.

It was easier when Father died, Clyde thought. Mother and I disliked him equally. Now, I have no one to share my dislike for my mother. He walked to his car, leaving the smell of diesel fumes from the train behind as he faced the exhaust from exiting vehicles.

The Bathroom on the Train

Clyde walked to his car, desperately telling himself not to escape to those food places tonight. There was only one solution.

"I'm going to believe in hope. I am not what my mother created. I need to find someone to tell this to and stop being lonely. Maybe I'll tell someone on the train tomorrow. Maybe one of those commuters who looks lonely like me."

As Clyde approached his car, he noticed another parked car three spaces away. A smallish woman he knew from the train leaned against the front hood of her car writing something in a dark blue notebook. A few weeks ago on the evening train, he overheard her talking to another woman about art. He remembered her name was Angie.

He wanted to say something to her, like how he was not always into self-pity and fatness. Clyde wanted to tell her about his bathroom incident and laugh with her over it. As he approached, she looked up and smiled.

Except, he had to rush home and pee.

The Back of the Seat

As the evening commuter train pulled away from the station, Angie slipped out of her heels to ease her suffering feet. She wished she had remembered her flats. The train did not care about her feet as it continued south.

She got her window seat by spending money and time to commute north via Metrorail. That way she could board the train at the first station before it headed south. It added to her commute, but she had the first pick of seats. By the time the train got to her regular station, empty seats would be scarce. There would be none in this popular train car for her ex-husband who wanted to be her husband again.

In the three years since he left, David's relationships had included women sporting thin eyebrows. That fashion was so overrated, Angie thought. A month ago, he began getting on the evening train at her station and sitting with her. Now when he got on, she could always count on another commuter sitting next to her. Seat made unavailable to her ex.

As the train came out of a short tunnel, Angie scooted down and propped her knees against the back of the seat before her. The surface was hard enough not to annoy the person sitting in that seat, but flexible enough to allow her to remain like this. She felt comfortable, at least for the moment.

This position caused Angie's brown stretch slacks to tug at her hips. She became quickly irritated with her body fat holding onto the morning's sugar donut as if no more was coming. She tried to forget the pull on her slacks as the train's click-clack rose in frequency.

Outside her window, Angie spied, like she spied every evening, a small church steeple sitting between tall office buildings. She saw the little church as a survivalist, much like herself. Dropping her feet to the floor, she pulled out her dark blue notebook to write about it. Instead, she found what she wrote yesterday evening at home.

"I believe in myself," David said to me after following me off the train.

"You believe yourself to be something other than what you really are," I told him.

She wrote this exchange of words in her journal to make sure her memory was accurate. Ugh, Angie thought. I should rip out these pages. I don't want to immortalize a man with a Jekyll and Hyde personality who is more Hyde than Jekyll. I want my notebook filled with only heroic, wonderful events and not the bad choices and feats of cowardice I had when chasing after for a happy ending.

At the next station, a short man with long feet sat next to Angie. Playing his video game with earphones on, it seemed he would not notice if the train was a rocket ship headed for Mars. At the third stop, more commuters filled the remaining seats, leaving nothing for her ex who would be waiting at the fourth stop.

During these stops, Angie wrote in her blue notebook, *"The diesel engine moves across truss bridges and steel tracks with noise and weight, pulling metal boxes filled with bouncy, fleshy bodies. My fellow passengers are a herd of headaches and tired backs swaying to the click-clack movement inside long metal canisters."*

She looked up for more inspiration at the commuters she shared breathing air with. Being short, mostly she saw only the back of seats. Angie turned to look out the darkening train window and saw her reflection.

There was no paleness to her splotchy skin and no color to her dark brown hair. But her eyebrows were full. Her reflection made her look younger than a thirty-one-year-old commuter surrounded by backs of the seats.

Angie continued writing in her notebook with sentences ending in exclamation points, question marks, or beginning with *"I remember once..."* A smile crossed her face or it folded into a frown, depending on what thoughts made up her mind.

The fourth stop came and went. David was somewhere, like a ghost trying to haunt her. She went back to her writing as other stations came and went. Sometimes writing with random thoughts and other times she worked on her play she hoped would one day be produced. Every few minutes, she pushed against her back of the seat. It felt good to stretch against something firm, solid, and strong while the back of the seat before her became something to focus on.

Eventually her seatmate left and, like a vampire, her ex swooped in. He dropped his pudgy butt into the vacated seat like he was ready to suck the life out of her. Not wanting him to see what she wrote, Angie packed her blue notebook in the yellow satchel at her feet.

She did not look at him, but said, "I'm not in your book of who's who that lets you continue to know me."

"Age is catching up to me. I want to know why we can't get back together," said David.

Sitting quietly in her train seat, Angie faced her window where flashes and blurred shapes of lighted, stationary buildings and street lamps flickered past. She wished she could pass that quickly from this man's attention. He continued to fill the air between them with noise and she continued to stare out the window.

With thin hands and fingers folded neatly in her lap, Angie was not wholly conscious of the moving train or his words. Yet, he kept talking and the train kept moving.

"I can't be bothered with you anymore," Angie said, turning toward him. "And, we can't be sitting like this together anymore." She narrowed her round eyes and furrowed her brow into a clear indication she wanted him to go away.

"Don't you want to give me a second chance? Don't you want me to make it up to you?" His voice sounded tinny.

"I touched your chapped lips in winter and smelled your sweat in summer. Then you ran away when I was at my weakest." Angie straightened herself against the back of the seat for strength. These were good, durable seat backs, she thought.

"You dumped mortality on me," David said. "I couldn't deal with it. What happened to you wasn't fair to me."

"I'm the one who had the cancer. You had no sympathy or caring for me." Angie dug through her purse and took out a small makeup case.

"Your cancer scared me."

"It's not contagious. It's what it is. It was just an excuse for you to leave."

"I don't like this talk. Let's change the subject and let me tell you about how I changed."

Angie touched her forehead and chin with tan powder out of the dusty case so she could concentrate on something rather than her ex sitting beside her talking about changes. The makeup kept her from looking old and gave her hope that maybe one day someone else would love her. In the compact mirror, she surveyed the lines on her face she refused to call wrinkles.

To shut David up, she said, "You used to say we were a book to be written. Yet, you found other chapters to write."

"Yeah, I went with other women. I found out they're all alike. Not you. You're different. You wear too much makeup and pull on your hair a lot. With these women, I reached for it all. You should be happy I realized you're the one I need."

To the man Angie used to have feelings for, she said, "We're not a couple anymore. I can't depend on you, ever."

As was her trait, Angie looked at one blue eye of his, then the other. She could not help being indecisive about which one to focus on. She spoke quickly to stop her eyes' dance, "This is my rule: I insist there is a final *gone* between us."

He gave a sly, intoxicating smile that caused her to look away. Her command finished and her point missed. She did not want to have feelings for him. Angie looked out the train window and saw only her reflection against the darkness. She rested her head against the back of the seat as chaos reigned in her head. She wished for someone to stay warm with and harbor in for a long stay. Could people she had loved change? Focus, focus, she thought.

She told David, "I'll have someone else to love one day. You're in my past and that person will be in my future."

David let loose a smile like the Cheshire Cat. "We once shared a life together and we can do it again. I can be your past and your future."

Angie did not want this discussion to continue. She wanted to know who these other commuters were she rode with every day. Did they know about her life? These others wallow with me in this twilight between home and work, heading toward undefined contests at both ends, and all anyone sees is the backside of someone else's seat. Angie thought this while looking at her thin fingers not expressing these thoughts in her notebook.

The train slowed toward their station. Angie gathered up her bag, ignoring whatever David was saying, as the train came to a sharp stop. The motion caused them to lean forward together. They got up, without touching, and concentrated on following other commuters through the narrow exit. Other commuters who lived their lives somewhere besides a commuter train, Angie thought.

She followed the queue off the train and spied Phil several people ahead. He looked confused as always. Angie wondered if his lips were chapped and what his sweat smelled like. He looked like someone who would have moist lips and sweat that did not smell like sweat.

Standing on the station platform, the sounds and noise of the train's moving metal faded away. Angie waited for her ex to leave the parking lot and instead watched Phil drive away. Around her, the loud stormy motion of the commuter train receded into the surrounding darkness, leaving her alone under a halogen lamp with restless, chilly air moving in.

David came back from the parking lot after seeing Angie on the platform. "I thought you were behind me," he said.

"Why would I follow you? I don't need your companionship anymore. I need to get back on this train in the morning and continue with my life," Angie said, twisting in her high heels. She walked away, making her shoes slap loudly against the concrete. Her feet hurt doing this, but it had a dramatic effect to her.

"I'll see you tomorrow," he said to her back.

She turned, fantasizing him as a vampire and she holding a stake. "I need something strong to keep me from falling backward. There's no back to you."

Angie spun around when he drew his hand over his head and gave a floppy goodbye wave. As much as she wished they could reunite, they would only spiral back into old habits. A commuter train may get new cars, but the points there and back remained the same, she thought.

Angie walked to her car thinking about what she would write in her journal when she got home. Maybe about how the back of seat she faced and the one she put her back against gave her strength to continue commuting.

Commuting Agendas

Danny listened to violin concertos on the commute out of the city. It was Friday evening and the music helped him relax as he looked forward to the weekend. When he got home, his pregnant daughter Beatrice met him in the foyer.

The coming birth gave them something to say to each other. Her protruding stomach kept them from saying too much.

"I need a car loan. Will you sign for it or should I list you as deceased?" Twenty-year-old Beatrice being Beatrice.

She blocked her dad's way into the house and prevented him from reaching his cold supper. Danny asked her, "Why don't you ask your boyfriend to sign for the loan?" He refrained from adding, *Yeah, the one who got you pregnant.*

"You know he's gone. He's looking for a job."

Danny was hungry and tired and unsure of Beatrice's mental state. He didn't want to challenge her fantasy that her boyfriend was looking for a job. They both knew the boyfriend had found a hang out with friends and was enjoying another alcohol/drug induced binge.

Dropping his backpack into the corner, Danny sighed once, heavily, before saying, "I get up early so I can get to work early so I can get home early so I can go to bed early. Yet, I'm always coming home late and going to bed late and getting up early comes too soon in the morning."

"Your bedroom door is not an escape. When you close yourself inside, I know you're still in there," Beatrice said with hands on hips and short legs pressed apart, searching for balance. Her round belly looked like she was growing the head of another Beatrice.

"Like I was trying to explain to you, I'm in my bedroom trying to get more than five hours of sleep."

"Mom understands me better than you and she commutes, too. I don't see why you don't drive together so you don't have to take that slow train all the time."

Danny's life flashed before him the last time he rode with his wife Piper in rush hour traffic. She drove like they were back in India where they grew up. Their parents gave them American names to stand out among their classmates in India, which did not help with their schooling or Piper's driving. Danny knew one day that statistics would prove she was the reason for all the bad rush hour traffic.

"Never mind, I'll list you as deceased for the loan," Beatrice said and stomped away.

Danny didn't get a chance to ask how a dead person could get a car loan. Things must be desperate out there in the banking world, he concluded, when dead people were more valuable than the living. He worried about why Beatrice was trying to get her own car.

The next morning on Saturday, Danny drove Piper and himself on a two-lane road toward the intersection of Route 50. It was a day trip to get out of the house and away from a moody, pregnant daughter. At least this was his excuse.

On the drive and to his right were open pastures sectioned

into unequal squares by rows of tall trees and low shrubs. Danny recognized Angus, Holstein, and Jersey cattle. In front of him the land sloped upward to create a happy looking, green mountain that reached gently toward a sky blue sky.

Before reaching Route 50, Danny followed a road sign to the left and detoured to Paris, Virginia. They rode a boring, narrow road without sidewalks that led them past bumps of federal style houses standing a few feet from the road's edge. Short, narrow, manicured lawns pretended to offer a barrier from cars. No people. Maybe the cows lived there, thought Danny. He didn't see a duplicative of the Eiffel Tower.

He found Route 50, a four-lane road west to Winchester where he would find a merlot to help remove the thought of returning home. An hour later at a downtown wine deli, Danny announced to Piper, "This is where I think we should live." Their wine glasses sat empty on a dark wooden bar.

"You want to live in a wine deli? Well, all right. I like it here, too."

"Stop kidding. I mean on one of those farms we passed on the way here."

"What's wrong with where we live now?" Piper let her thick brown hair tumble against her empty glass as she faced Danny with upturned dark eyebrows.

"We live there. We should live out here with farm animals."

"If you want a pet, we'll get a dog or maybe a bird, but no pigs or chickens. The neighbors might complain."

Ignoring Piper's joke, Danny continued, "It's just that we keep commuting between the same two places every day. If we want to break out and become someone else, we can't because we exist in a stable world without animals."

"I don't want to be someone else. I've been working on this self of mine all my life and I think I'm finally getting somewhere with it." Piper slipped off her barstool, intending to go some place else.

Danny followed his wife outside into the part of the downtown where cars were not allowed. They found an ice cream shop with blue and yellow flags in front. He had a small cup of chocolate chocolate chocolate ice cream. Piper was braver holding a sugar cone of blueberry vanilla cherry ice cream.

"I feel happy in these mountains," said Danny, watching people walk around.

"If we move here, Beatrice and her baby may come with us," Piper said with emphasis that their troubles would not be left behind.

Danny noticed Piper didn't mention the absent father.

"That's the point. I want them to come. I think it will be good for all of us to get away from commuting. I want my granddaughter to learn how to milk a cow."

"Cows kick."

"You kick sometimes in bed. I survive," said Danny.

"Let's see if you survive my kick tonight." Piper gave her husband a wink.

He wiped the ice cream off her chin.

In the following weeks, they did not talk about moving. Instead, the three of them rushed headlong towards the birth of their grandchild with a baby shower and repeated medical appointments. Minor concerns vocalized, yet dismissed by the medical community, made Danny wonder if medical professionals had lost their ability to be people. Instead of listening more carefully to the tiny heartbeat in Beatrice's stomach, he witnessed their townhouse get smaller with baby items.

Baby Tres came on a cloudy, cool Friday morning. The newborn stayed wrapped in hospital blankets and did not breathe for way too many seconds. When she did breathe, those seconds had been costly. She was incubated. No one on the hospital staff was free of furrowed brows and hurried whispers.

Beatrice's boyfriend came that Monday after staying with friends on a binge that ended when their binge supply ran out. By Wednesday, Beatrice and he had moved their stuff and baby's things, without the baby, into the refurbished garage that acted as a home-to-be.

Danny disliked the boyfriend more than he disliked commuting. Much more. Danny refused to say the boyfriend's name as if it was the worst of foul words. The boyfriend understood this when he told Danny he would marry Beatrice after the hospital released Tres.

For the rest of the week, Beatrice stayed at the hospital watching Tres surrounded by worried professional equipment. When the father was there, he hung out with the nurses. Danny and Piper came and went like grandparents did, trying to believe everything would be all right.

After living for a week, Tres died alone on a sunny morning when her mother went to the bathroom and her father ran away from the alarms, never to be seen again.

The news came to Danny and Piper in text messages from medical staff where the auto correct wouldn't change reality. The messages were like the beginning of a dystopian novel. Danny and Piper got to the hospital after Beatrice finally convinced a nurse to take her picture holding the dead Tres. Danny vowed to destroy that picture one day.

The medical community took the baby away as if she was never there. While Piper held Beatrice, Danny went looking for Tres.

He didn't understand why the morgue had more security than the rest of the hospital. Dead Tres had more protection than live Tres. Danny had a lot of security people escort him to his wife and daughter, but no one to protect them for what came after.

The funeral happened on Monday. For all that following week, the train ran on time. Except Danny was not on it. He stayed home with Piper and Beatrice so they all could avoid the garage full of baby things and not talk about what happened. A week after Tres died, Danny got up at four in the morning and went into the garage where he listened to the empty crib. Maybe Tres did not want to live with a commuting family, he told the crib.

On Saturday morning at breakfast, Beatrice announced she was writing a short story to avoid conversations between them about baby things. Danny didn't remember any conversations.

"The story is about a train commuter who enjoys dancing. I think Tres would have liked to dance."

"You used to like to dance." Danny tried to focus on his scrambled eggs. They sat at the kitchen table waiting for the coffee to finish making.

"Maybe I will one day. Right now, I'm collaborating with Mom on the story."

That sounded even worse, Danny thought. His wife walked in and he left without his coffee or eggs, not wanting to hear about their collaboration.

For the next two weeks, commuting became a timely, mundane event that left Danny plagued with memories of who Tres could have been. He had hoped to take her back to India so she could visit her relatives. He wanted to go back anyway, but Piper and Beatrice were working on their short story.

Almost a month after the funeral, Beatrice got a job in the

same direction as her parents. She drove them in her new car using Tres' death as collateral. Danny could not understand how someone dead could be held in collateral. Particularly, someone who only lived a week. He concluded that the banking institution was made up of people who had no beliefs and were unhappy.

On the way home one evening, Danny sat in front with Beatrice driving. Piper slept in the backseat. Beatrice told her father, "Everyone has scars—superficial, deep, and biting."

"What does that mean? Is that in your short story?" Danny wondered if Tres' death was changing Beatrice into something other than who she had been.

"I never believed my tears were real until now." Beatrice stared out the side window.

Beatrice might have been crying. Danny did not look. He decided Beatrice was repeating what was in the short story. He grabbed the steering wheel so they would avoid hitting a commuter bus. His daughter was a lot like her mother when driving, Danny decided.

"The real purpose in life is to be happy. When a person fails in that, they fail at life," said Beatrice, returning to her driving.

"That all sounds good to be in your story," said Danny, who wanted it to be true. Otherwise, he wasn't sure about Beatrice's mental state.

They were silent the rest of the way home. After supper, the three of them sat at the kitchen table deciding to carpool together with Beatrice's new car since they all ended up in the same place, anyway. Actually, Beatrice and Piper decided this. Danny volunteered to drive since having mother and daughter drive would make the traffic news too often.

On Fridays, they rode the train since this was the day Tres

died and there was no other reason except they felt this way.

One Friday evening on the train, Beatrice announced, "Tres' ghost wants us to keep riding the rails." She explained how a chill shivered up her nape and it was a sign they should keep riding the train. Danny was glad since, in the past few weeks, they missed being in two car accidents. Driving in rush hour traffic with drivers of erratic personalities created a lot of risk, even for Danny.

Soon after this decision, Piper and Beatrice co-published their short story in a popular Irish magazine for no pay and all three visited that country two months later. The Irish people were pleasant talkers and, for the most part, happy.

Everything was green and wet with short, narrow roads running closely past low thatched roofs that these mostly happy people lived in. Bright blues and yellows made the small towns look like smiles. Danny liked the Guinness beer and pub sandwiches. Wherever they went, they were never late because they had no schedule to keep.

On the last day, they stood in front of castle remains listening to a tour guide explain about the occupants' deaths centuries ago. Nearby, Piper saw a black and white cow lying in a pasture of short grass. Three red birds sat on the cow's long backbone like they had always known each other. Piper told Danny she wanted a cow when they went home.

"It's not legal where we live. Besides, a cow is pretty big as a pet," said Danny. He tried to imagine where in their house a cow would sleep.

"Those animals seem very stable and I think commuting is too risky," Piper said.

He didn't know what cows and commuting had to do with each other. But he agreed about the risk of commuting, despite riding a commuter train.

Piper said, "There's a lot of rock near Winchester."

Most of the rocks in Ireland had become decaying castles.

Four months later, Danny cashed out his retirement, figuring his job and commuting would guarantee his death long before he retired. He and Piper moved to an eleven-acre farm between Paris and Winchester where they bought seven Holstein cows, six goats, and five llamas. Piper refurbished furniture and Danny sold polished rocks he found on the farm as jewelry.

Beatrice moved into a condo next to the train station and continued to commute by train. She visited her parents every weekend and helped with farm life. One Sunday before she drove back to her condo, she told her parents, "I'd live out here with you two, but I think Tres has plans for me. I need to continue riding the commuter train to find out what they are. Maybe I'll find out in the next story I write."

Carolyn and Beatrice

Carolyn stood on a concrete platform waiting with other commuters for a train to take her away from where she stood. She hoped her infant daughter Alice would not be commuting like this when she grew up. After riding the train to her new job the past few months, Carolyn had more sympathy for her dad Tony, who was still train commuting after all these years.

When the train came, Carolyn followed the crowd up wide metal stairs and through a sliding pocket door where she confronted the longness of the train car. Peering around wide male bodies for an available seat, she spied a young woman in an aisle seat. Her position prevented anyone from reaching the empty window seat.

Balding men approached this woman and pointed at the empty seat, intending her to scoot out of the way. She ignored them by staring into the back of the seat before her. They shuffled away, probably thinking it had been too long a day to fight it out with a crazy woman. Maybe this woman would meet a man who still had fight left in him, but not before Carolyn got there. When she did, the woman moved her wide hips and swung her legs out in one fluid motion, opening the window seat for Carolyn to sit in. The invitation appeared too easy, but Carolyn was tired and other seats were filling up fast.

"Men are arrogant and they smell," said the woman.

Carolyn did not have the energy for conversation and did not reply. The woman smelled like stale roses.

"Men spread their legs and elbows trying to look big. It only makes them look smaller. You get off at the same stop I do."

Carolyn wasn't sure whether it was a question or a statement of fact. She could not remember who got off at her stop. Even she forgot to get off at her stop sometimes.

"I'm Beatrice and my parents used to ride the train with me. But they moved away."

Carolyn felt pressured to say something. "I'm Carolyn. Sometimes I ride with my dad, but often he takes a later train or an earlier train. Actually, he takes the train I'm not riding. We see each other a lot at home."

"Your mother doesn't ride the train?"

"She died." Carolyn wished she had not said it that directly, or at all. She must have been more tired than she thought. It sounded like she didn't care anymore about her mom's death, although she had been thinking too much about her lately.

"My daughter Tres died six months ago. She was only a week old and never got a chance to leave the hospital."

The train jerked to a start and headed south. Carolyn did not like how things got so serious so fast. "I'm sorry. That is very hard losing your newborn."

"I guess you're wondering about Tres' father."

"No, not really." Carolyn really didn't.

"He ran away, never to be seen again. He would have run away even if Tres had lived. With him gone, I planned to devote myself to Tres. But she went away, too."

"What about your parents?" Carolyn wanted a different subject.

"I was living with them when Tres died. Maybe her death helped them decide to move to the mountains. They wanted me to come, too, but I felt that if I left I would be leaving Tres behind. She only lived at the hospital, so I got a condo near there in case her spirit was looking for me. Maybe that's not right. I feel like I'm still learning all this. You have children?"

"I have a little girl, Alice. Her father decided she was not his child. Like you, I'm glad he left. The next guy I get involved with will be more mature. At least I hope so."

"I got a nurse to take a picture of Tres before they took her to the morgue."

"Why did you take a photo after . . . ?" Carolyn hunted for polite words.

"I had to have something to remember her by. The nurses wrapped her up and she looks like she's asleep. I'll show you." The woman dug around in her pocketbook.

Carolyn wanted to look at anything other than the photograph of a dead newborn. She searched in her wide purse and picked out her smartphone. But it needed charging. With a frown, she put it back and wished she had a book to read or something to look at that didn't need charging.

Beatrice pulled out the photograph and held it in her hands like it was a precious gem. The photo seemed like it floated toward Carolyn. The last time she saw an actual photograph was in an antique store. Carolyn wanted a reason to look away from the photo. She studied the heavy, tall man in the seat across the aisle who was trying hard to take up less space, yet his size prevented it.

"Is your dad the one looking for a ghost's emerald ring?" Beatrice asked, waiting for Carolyn to look at the photograph.

"Yeah, how did you know?" Carolyn worried about Beatrice's intentions.

"Cheryl the conductor told me. She was telling me how she was helping your dad, although I don't know why. I think Cheryl just likes mysteries and ghosts."

Carolyn needed to talk to her dad about talking too much on the train.

"I met a woman on the train who thought her Catalan great grandfather Luis was haunting her. She sounded crazy." Beatrice waved her photograph in the air as if swatting away all the ghosts. "I once thought Tres was haunting the train, but I don't think that's true. Why would my daughter hang around a commuter train? I think she may be haunting me in a good way, like a guardian angel. You think your dad and my parents ever met?"

"I don't know. He doesn't talk a lot about people he meets. At least not after he got a dog."

"What's the dog's name?"

"Mary. It was my mom's name." Carolyn cringed. She wished she had not said this.

"That says a lot."

"Where in the mountains did your parents move to?" Carolyn was desperate to change the subject.

Beatrice dropped the photo into her handbag assuming, Carolyn had finished looking at it. "They wanted to escape from this commute and bought an eleven-acre farm between Paris and Winchester. To keep them company, they bought some cows, goats, and a few llamas. My mother refurbishes old furniture and makes cheeses from the cow and goat milk. I don't think Llamas make milk, at least not for cheeses. My dad has a mini-manufacturing plant in the basement where he polishes stones to sell at a flea market and online. He makes more than when he was working at a company."

"Sounds a lot better than commuting."

"They talked about moving out there before Tres' death and her dying may have convinced them to do it. Or it could have been the commute. Either way, I can't blame them for seeing their mortality. I'm having a hard time seeing anything after giving birth to my daughter wrong."

Carolyn looked around for an empty seat to escape the dead baby talk. There was no chance of getting another seat as people were standing in the aisle. Plus, she would have to crawl over Beatrice to get out. "It looks like we're going to be sitting together for a while. Let's pace ourselves with our tragedies."

"Sorry. It gets out of me sometimes," said Beatrice. "I've been talking to this woman, Paula. She told me about an artist group made up of only women. I should probably look into joining."

"I know Paula. Her artist group seems like it'd be a lot of fun." Carolyn promised had herself to ask for an invitation. She wondered if they'd let her bring Alice if she brought Mary along, too. Probably. Happy dogs were usually welcomed and Alice was quiet with Mary around.

"Mary is always waiting for you at the train station."

"Yeah, she walks the two miles through the woods when the weather is good. At least she's smart enough to stay out of bad weather. We tried keeping her in the house, but she's a good escape artist," said Carolyn.

"Tres would have liked your dog. Maybe she wouldn't have died if I had a dog for her waiting at home. If I had a dog, I would have called him Joe, even if it was a she. I'd tell Joe about Tres and they would have been friends, if she had lived and if I had a dog."

Carolyn considered getting off at the next stop and catching the next train. However, Beatrice knew where she got off. Carolyn asked, "Are you talking to anyone about the loss of your daughter?"

"I'm talking to you."

Carolyn let out a heavy sigh.

"I'm considering making a list of all the train people I've talked to about Tres." Beatrice stared at the back of the seat before her, maybe looking for answers in the fabric.

Carolyn did not want her name added to the list. She already heard about a woman asking to see baby pictures because she couldn't have children. These two women were using the train as a means of therapy, Carolyn thought. The train company could make a lot of money hiring a psychiatrist.

"I'm sorry, but I've had a long day. I'm going to close my eyes for a few minutes." Carolyn envied the people standing in the aisle. They were better off standing than sitting next to Beatrice. Carolyn wished her backpack held a bottle of chardonnay or a merlot to get her through this commute.

"I'm sorry about showing you the photo," Beatrice said. "If I didn't say she was dead, people would probably look at it happily."

Carolyn felt guilty for not being sympathetic. "I think it would be worse if they looked, then you told them. Maybe you should just keep the photo to yourself."

"You like piano music?"

Carolyn remembered the upright in Alice's room. Her dad bought the piano saying he wanted to learn how to play because Mary seemed to like music and he always wanted to learn. That was Mary the dog and not her mother's ghost, her dad explained. Carolyn wondered.

"Yeah. Music is supposed to help with a baby's development," Carolyn said, although Alice seemed to be developing better with Mary around.

"I don't think so. They had a piano on the hospital floor. I don't know why. Someone was playing a children's song as Tres was dying."

Carolyn vowed to be more careful who she sat with from now on.

"I guess the music was for those babies who lived," Beatrice said, letting out a shallow sigh.

Carolyn said, "I can't imagine how it is to lose your child." Alice was everything to Carolyn.

Beatrice leaned back looking for strength in the back of the seat she pushed against. "I'm so stupid to unload on you like this. Let's change the subject. Tell me about your dog Mary."

Carolyn let out a sigh of relief. "She's a beagle and acts too human to be a dog. She's always happy and Alice loves her."

"Is Mary the dog helping your dad find the emerald ring ghost? I was wondering if I should help, too. Cheryl is already helping."

"I don't know about looking for ghosts on the train. But if there were ghosts, Mary would find them."

"You think I should move in with my parents near the mountains?" Beatrice acted like she forgot about Mary.

"I don't know." Carolyn did not want to be this involved in Beatrice's life.

"I don't know, either. If I had a dog named Joe, I'd hope he or she would help me decide. You think Mary can help me decide? Your dog, not your mom."

Carolyn thought Mary could do that, but it would mean further commitment and obligation in Beatrice's life. "No, I don't think so," lied Carolyn.

They had several moments of silence until Beatrice said, "Sorry, but I've had a long day and all this thinking has worn me out. I'm going to take a nap. Please wake me up before our stop." Beatrice scooted down in her seat and slipped her head back. She was asleep in a few moments.

Carolyn knew because she started snoring. One of those gurgling, getting louder snores that brought stares from passengers who wanted Carolyn to do something about it. They gave her the look that they knew Beatrice had saved the seat for her.

Shocked at how fast Beatrice went to sleep, Carolyn ignored the stares. They didn't know Beatrice like she knew her in the short time they rode together. Carolyn let Beatrice snore away until just before their stop.

She nudged Beatrice awake and gave her a tissue to wipe the drool off her chin. They said nothing as Beatrice led the way off the train and down the wide metal stairs. When they stepped onto the concrete platform, Mary sat at the far end looking like she knew the secrets of the universe and wasn't telling anyone.

Behind her was a dirt path that ran parallel to the tracks before turning under a bridge and toward the townhouse community. The path held the remnants of the forest that lived prior to the train tracks, parking lot, and houses. This time, Mary sat next to a mixed breed dog with long fur and a long, heavy tail that wagged like it was going to fly off. Whatever mixed breed the dog was, it was certainly all of the larger kinds. The strange dog ran into Beatrice's arms as she kneeled down to accept all the licks.

"Mary found me a dog," Beatrice said, not caring who she told this to.

The stray had no collar or identification and looked like it had been without a home for several days. Carolyn carried Mary to her car, leaving Beatrice and her new friend to go home in the other direction.

The next evening, Carolyn settled in an aisle seat next to a wide man who tried to take up less seat space. A few minutes after the train started south, Cheryl the conductor knelt beside Carolyn.

"This is my last day as a conductor."

Carolyn wondered why Cheryl told her this. Was it about dad's emerald ring ghost?

"This is not about your dad's ghost thing. This is about you letting Beatrice snore on the train yesterday evening. A lot of people have been rude to her."

"Thanks, but I didn't mind."

"I wanted you to know that Beatrice and I have been seeing each other since her baby died."

"That's great." Carolyn didn't think letting Beatrice snore was enough to build this much trust.

"You helped Beatrice find that dog Joe."

"Actually, my dad's dog Mary found Joe." Carolyn thought credit should go to whom it deserved. Or blame.

"I had been trying to get Beatrice to move in with me and Joe showing up was the sign that convinced her."

Carolyn believed in signs. "I'm glad for the two of you." She really was. She was also glad that maybe Beatrice might stop showing Tres' photograph to people.

"We won't see each other again. My dad helped Beatrice and me buy a bed-and-breakfast near Paris, Virginia. It's going to be pet friendly. Also, one last thing."

Carolyn noticed several nearby commuters had paused their electronics to listen.

"The green wine bottle on the bridge is gone. I think that

wind storm we had a few weeks ago blew it off the ledge. Your dad doesn't have to look for the emerald ring anymore."

That evening at the kitchen table, Carolyn asked her dad about the bottle being gone.

"I think it was haunting me. I could see it each evening as the train crossed the bridge. I'm glad it's gone because it means that the 1969 ghost is gone, too. If we need anything, your mother's spirit will help us."

"I don't think she ever went away," Carolyn said, looking at Mary the dog.

Months later, Carolyn got an email from Beatrice and Cheryl. They adopted a son they named Charlie who they said looked a lot like Tres. They were happy not to be commuting.

Morning Commute

Claudia woke up thinking of a dream about her great grandpapa Luis. Fleeting images came and went concerning her father's grandfather, a Catalan who fought in the Spanish Civil War.

In her dream, he had reached out to her with his calloused hand and she had turned away from him. She stayed awake, not wishing to know anymore from her great grandpapa who was telling her in the dream about important things such as loyalty and compassion. Lying in bed next to her husband Ernie, Claudia remembered the stories she heard as a child about him.

He lived in Barcelona as the Nationalists invasion started the Spanish Civil War. He sided with the Republic until Franco's Army of Africa and the Nationalists started winning battles, then he changed sides. Luis changed sides again and rejoined the Republic when they won the first battles for Madrid. Over the years, family members told how Luis thought that was how it should be in a civil war. You stayed with the winning side. Yet, he changed sides so often he sometimes forgot whether or not he was on Franco's side. He did not want to gamble, and he followed the vacating Abe Lincoln brigade of Americans to the U.S. as they fled with the anarchists.

Like her great grandpapa, Claudia had a hard time staying loyal to any one side in a marriage for very long. Maybe that was why she tried to explain *seny* and *rauxa* to Ernie last night at supper.

"Are they Russian or French words?"

"They're Catalan terms. *Seny* means 'common sense' and *rauxa* is 'madness.' They seem to describe my life so far."

"You seem to think you have some connection with your great grandfather that you don't. He died before you were born and I don't think he would bother haunting you."

"Why not? I'm hauntable. You just don't see things like I do. You know what? I really don't care." Claudia left the table. She was getting angry and did not want to blurt out some truth about herself that should be kept secret.

That morning in bed, Claudia looked at the clock. It was a few minutes before the alarm went off, so she turned off the alarm and got up. She stepped onto a shag rug that should have been plusher. After two years of marriage to Ernie, they were still living in an apartment with a cheap rug. She had thought he would be rich by now and they would be living in a Victorian house with oak floors and Persian rugs. It aggravated her.

While Ernie slept, Claudia shuffled into the bathroom with a sour taste in her mouth that felt like a bad lie if it could be felt: bitter, stale, and dry. Lying gets easier the more you get away with it, she thought. In the shower, the tiny rivulets of hot water abused her skin, and she remembered two months ago when she and Ernie were coming home from their beach vacation.

"When did you get a tattoo?" Ernie had a feminine pitch to his voice when angry. He finally noticed the tattoo after

Claudia lowered the V neck of her white blouse to expose the red bull on her breast.

Ernie's head jerked from her tattooed breast, to the traffic, and back at least four times. Claudia eagerly braced for the sudden impact of crunching metal and ballooning air bags that never came. He was such a safe driver.

"I did it for you, darling," Claudia lied. She wanted to get Ernie angry. "It had to be done or I would have had a dull vacation."

They argued over the tattoo for ten minutes before falling silent the rest of the long, three-hour drive back home.

Claudia remembered this as she finished showering and stood before the bathroom mirror. She evaluated the tattoo of the red bull sitting across her left breast. Claudia wished it had more red. She pushed her breast up to let the bull's broad, red chest explode outward. A great addition to my body, she thought. She reviewed the rest of her heavy body that was not obese. It's just enough flesh to like myself, she believed. After all, I am all there is to me.

Claudia faced the bathroom mirror and let out a bored sigh while pushing mousse through her thick hair. The white streaks reminded her of ocean white caps. Two months ago when they were at the beach and before the tattoo, Claudia remembered lying on a striped towel on a wide, crowded beach.

On her back with her head propped up and her bare feet facing the ocean, she looked at Ernie standing waist deep in the blue green water. The fool never learned to swim, unlike my great grandpapa Luis, who could have probably swum across the Atlantic Ocean if he wanted.

As she worked with her thick hair in the bathroom, Claudia thought about the men who stopped by her area of sand to say obvious things. She let men examine her body, like a piece of fat sirloin on a grill. Those men won't stop thinking of me, she thought. Young women nearby gave her evil stares. She enjoyed making them jealous.

Claudia paid more attention to a tall man with a cowboy hat and a tight-fitting swimsuit who brought his shadow across her. She kept her back flattened against the beach towel, looking up at his silhouette. It was like he had fallen across her body. Beneath her, the coarse hot sand pushed back through the towel.

She slipped away from this memory and called out to Ernie from the bathroom, "We should take a good long vacation next year."

"What are you talking about? We went to the beach for a week this summer," he said, climbing out of bed. Spending money always got him moving, she thought.

Claudia went into the bedroom's walk-in closet, not wanting to be in the bathroom with Ernie taking a shower. She roughed through her blouses before settling on a polyester blend of pale green that needed ironing. Her bra pinched tight against her ribs, making the cleavage look battered, but prominent. A dark blue cotton skirt over her hips was tight, but she vowed this was the last size she would graduate up to.

Like most mornings, Ernie and she finished in their respective enclosures and entered the bedroom at the same time, like fighters entering a ring. She had more work in the bathroom and he needed clothes from the closet. They passed each other without touching.

Ernie's spicy cologne lingered in the bathroom air as Claudia made final preparations with her hair. Some mornings, her hair settled on her head simply. Not this morning.

Claudia found Ernie at the kitchen table finishing his cereal. He looked like a kid getting ready for middle school. Without speaking, he put his bowl in the dishwasher and gathered his backpack. Claudia just needed her brown coat and pocketbook, since she would come back to the house after dropping him at the train station.

"I want to know more about my great grandpa Luis. I want to know about the romance of a Catalan Spain and the excitement of a civil war," Claudia said as she got in on the driver's side.

"You're talking crazy." Sitting in the cold front passenger seat, Ernie hugged his backpack to his chest.

"I want to take a trip to Spain next summer. I want to visit places like Barcelona where my great grandpapa grew up. I want to know more about him," Claudia told Ernie as she drove fast out of the apartment complex.

Ernie did not answer as he had one hand shoved against the dashboard and another clenching the door handle. Ahead of them, a pasture of fog hung in the road. It was a barrier Claudia plowed through, not caring what surprise could rise in the mist. She went fast and her high beams only showed glistening, heavy dew.

When the fog cleared enough for him to see more, Ernie said, "When are you going to get over your great grandfather? It's like you're obsessed with the man. You know, you had other relatives who were American."

"I don't care. I think I take after my great grandpapa Luis more than anyone else. I think he could be my guardian spirit. I want a long trip next year to Spain and I want it planned soon, so we're committed. I don't see why we can't just up and go places when I want to go."

"First, it's the money. Second, I don't know when I can get

off work next year."

"I work and I can get off anytime."

"You work part time and I don't see why you can't work full time. The company has been asking you to do that. Besides, you're taking me to the train already, so why don't you just go to work? What are you doing all morning back at the house, anyway?" Ernie blew a cloud of hot breath into the cold air between them.

"I'm up this early taking you to the train because we only have one car," Claudia said, taking a curve fast enough to squeal the tires.

"We only have one car because we can't afford another because you're only working part time." Ernie shifted in his seat, the old seat belt not helping much to hold him in place.

"I don't want to talk about it anymore. I'm doing the best I can. I want to go to Spain next year. I need to know more about my ancestry. If we plan now, we can afford it."

"We spent a week this summer at the beach in an expensive hotel. We have to pay that off first." Ernie sighed. Another cloud of his breath entered the car's compartment since it still had not warmed up enough to turn on the heat.

Claudia did not like seeing Ernie's breath hang around. It reminded her of how unexciting he was. I'll give him some excitement, she thought. Claudia slowed down as a car behind her blew its horn, anxious to get to the train. When she heard a train whistle in the distance, she sped up so she could make the train, barely.

Just before they got to the railroad crossing, the lights flashed red on the poles. Beside her, Ernie grabbed the dashboard again, this time with both hands. Claudia hit the ridge of the tracks as the bars began to lower. They bounced over the dual tracks like two bobble heads. Claudia wanted to giggle because she could picture them bouncing around like they were on an amusement ride.

She turned an immediate right into a parking lot and deliberately too close to a short woman bundled in an expensive looking overcoat. The woman jumped to the side, unsure of Claudia's intentions. She parked in front of a small wire fence that separated the car from the station platform. On the other side of the tracks, she saw the honking car didn't make the crossing. Claudia held down her laughter, not wanting to explain to Ernie why she was happy.

Ernie sat there not saying anything. Claudia could tell he was angry. She tried not to giggle. Making him like this was getting easier lately.

"This excites you, doesn't it?"

"*You* excite me, hon." Claudia enjoyed lying to her husband.

The roar of the approaching diesel engine stopped him from saying anything more. It didn't matter to Claudia because she had no plans to answer him. Ernie pushed his way out of the car, hesitated, and leaned his head through the doorway as the train rolled to a stop and the noise subsided.

"Try to be on time to pick me up. I've had to wait half an hour some evenings. You get off work early enough and you know when my train gets here. I don't see why you can't help me out a little and be on time for once."

"Sure, hon. I'll be here. Right on time. At least once."

Ernie stomped toward the train.

"He can't say things are dull living with me," Claudia told herself as she got out, too.

She leaned on the car's warm hood feeling like an expensive ornament. She wanted to understand Ernie, except she did not understand why she married him. Claudia suddenly feared that she did not understand love.

The sagging wire fence made some futile attempt at a barrier between the vehicles and commuter train. Ernie walked fast through an open gate and climbed into the first car at the front of the train. Through the large rectangular windows, she watched him walk the narrow aisles toward the back end of the train where he liked to sit.

She was glad she didn't have to ride a commuter train. They looked like boring people who didn't realize they rode in metal boxes looking like coffins.

In the train car where Ernie was headed, a lone passenger got off. This man wore a tall, wide brim hat and a starched white shirt with a black string tie dangling down his broad chest. He had a brass buckle on his leather belt and his tight denim jeans led down to rattlesnake boots. The picture of him standing against the dark suits and power ties of other men made Claudia slip her wet tongue across dry lips.

Ernie finally sat down in the same train car that the stranger got off. Claudia frowned and hoped Ernie did not sit in the same seat as the cowboy. She became nervous and anxious that the two men could be the same person who looked different.

Claudia knew Ernie was too angry to look at her leaning against the car's hood. She didn't care as she kept her eye on the cowboy who walked along the wire fence. As the train headed north, he stared at some part of Claudia's body. She didn't care where. It was his smirk that flooded her with tension, not the expected excitement of the previous few days.

He strode through the gate while Claudia twisted her wedding ring several times on her finger before pocketing it. Instantly, she felt unsure of what to do next. A stampede of confusion made her see the cowboy looking just as ordinary as Ernie.

Maybe it was the stumble the cowboy made coming through the gate. Maybe it was because he did not look at her face. Maybe it was the lack of expression that made him feel like an old habit. Either way, she did not expect the quick let down. Claudia panicked and was afraid that if she took her eyes off the cowboy, she would easily forget what he looked like.

She remembered her dream and great grandpa Luis who shouted, "Common sense *seny* or madness *rauxa?*" Maybe the dream was really a nightmare.

The cowboy slipped into the car like he had done each day that week and sat in the warm spot made by Ernie's body minutes before.

Not knowing what else to do, after the train left Claudia drove back across the railroad tracks, feeling the bumps as dull and rough. The bouncing began a headache in the back of her head that she wished would get worse and numb her from feeling anything else. The cowboy talked like a gnat buzzing in her ear.

Claudia went the longer way to give herself more time to think about the romance of a Catalan Spain and the excitement of a civil war. She fantasized about living with her great grandpapa Luis in an alien place that imprisoned her in extremes. With her eyes closed, she imagined the excitement and danger where death could occur at any time. She opened her eyes before she drove off the road.

Claudia toyed with the idea of driving until the car ran out of gas. Just to see where she ended up. If she did, she would not be taking the cowboy along.

She stopped outside a strip mall. "Get out and go away."

He spoke, she did not listen. Claudia blew the car's horn until he jumped out. Leaving him behind, she drove away watching the sun come up, burn off the remaining fog, and dry up the dew making everything too clear.

After a few miles, she turned around and went back to the train station where she called her work and took the day off. Claudia walked around the train station, realizing it was a dull place with no train to catch. She found a deli nearby and spent the afternoon waiting for Ernie's train. At least I won't be late this time, she thought.

When his train came, Claudia told Ernie about the cowboy. Their conversation lasted as long as it took to get home.

"He was my *rauxa* and you are my *seny*," Claudia said, hoping Ernie understood. They stood in the kitchen where they rarely talked.

"Okay, so using your terms back at you, I see our marriage as *rauxa*. I don't want a crazy *rauxa* marriage. I prefer *seny* or some common sense in my life, like when I'm riding the train away from you."

"Be careful how you use my great grandpa's terms." Claudia resented Ernie's comments, like they were a threat to her family.

"I don't want to talk about this anymore. You have no respect for me. In the morning I'll take the train, but don't worry about picking me up in the evening. I won't be there."

In the morning after Ernie left via a taxi to catch the train, Claudia thought about how great grandpa Luis chased rauxa. She had to find seny.

Incident on Train 302

On a spring morning that did not require jackets for the first time that year, commuters clustered along the train station platform watching the diesel locomotive approach. The growing sunshine on the horizon and shedding of excess clothing had everyone in a festive mood. Until it was time to climb into crowded train cars to jobs outlined by windowless cubicles.

As Tony was about to step up into his usual train car, a short, slim man, maybe in his forties, pushed in front of him. This man wore a dark suit, dark tie, and a white shirt as if he disliked color. This impatient, colorless man stomped up the metal stairs with a flare of arrogance and an air of importance. Tony followed him, since people behind were pushing.

The train car had an upper section of prized single seats that other commuters had already filled. The bottom section had dual seats flanking both sides of the car, creating a narrow aisle down the center. On this level, commuters prized the window seats. People in the aisle seats had to tolerate being bumped by on-training or de-training commuters. Plus, if someone fell asleep they could end up on the floor. The floor looked dirty.

In the middle of the train car, the impatient man plopped down in the last remaining window seat. Tony did not want to sit beside someone who had stolen his prized seat. So, he sat across in an aisle seat next to a petite man who did not take up too much seat space.

Quickly, a woman aging into her late twenties sat beside the black and white dressed man and across the aisle from Tony. She wore a blunt cut to her straight dark hair and a beige dress with floral designs suitable for the improving change in weather. However, her high heels were out of place, since most women wore flats and changed at work.

She had a tinge of heaviness to her body that added to her beauty and made her seem proud of who she was. This proud woman had a look that she would rip off the face of anybody who disagreed with her. This was Tony's commute that morning as he opened his paperback.

Thirty minutes later as most commuters were well into their morning nap or preparing for their workday, the train switched tracks and the window seat stealing man slumped over onto the dark hair woman's shoulder. He did so gracefully, like he had gone to sleep and thought she was his pillow. The woman gave the top of his head a look like, "Are you kidding me?"

The look did not work since the man's head slipped off her shoulder and headed for her lap, face first. She threw her hands in the air and stumbled into the narrow aisle to get away from him. The man continued falling until he stretched across both seats like they were his, and right now they were.

"What the hell is wrong with you?" She punched the guy's shoulder without a response.

"I don't think he heard you," said the petite man next to Tony. He peered around Tony to get a better look.

The woman leaned over to take a closer look at the guy's face and let out an ear-blasting scream.

People turned, jumped, cussed, and peered over the tops of the high-back seats like gophers bobbing out of their nested holes. Overhead in the one-seat balcony section, heads leaned over the top railings and Tony hoped no one spilled drool on them as the woman screamed again.

Sitting across the narrow aisle from the unfolding drama, Tony faced the woman's firm butt. He hoped she didn't fart in his face as she let out another high-pitched scream, just to make sure everyone was awake, even in the other train cars.

"I know CPR," a bald man yelled from a few seats away.

The woman screamed again, this time announcing the guy was dead. Tony wondered how she knew. He was lost as to what the screaming could do to help the man if he had died. Meanwhile, the commuter train continued happily along on its schedule to the next station.

"I know CPR," said another man a few seats in the opposite direction. He had a belly that looked like he had swallowed a basketball.

As both CPR men approached from opposing directions, the train switched tracks again and the screaming woman lost her balance. She stumbled backward and stuck a high heel into the soft part of the shoe worn by the balding CPR man.

He yelped like a little boy and jerked his foot away, causing more unbalancing to the screaming woman. She stumbled in the other direction and into the approaching CPR man with the belly. The two ended up on the dirty floor. The screaming woman on top, still hollering.

With her butt finally out of the way, Tony got a good view of the guy's head. It lolled around on the edge of the vinyl seat, keeping time with the train's rollicking movement like the beat of a slow jazz tune. The cheeks, forehead, and lips showed a shocking lack of blood color. Tony could not bring himself to do anything but stare at the pale face getting paler.

"Get off me. I've got to save that guy," said the CPR belly man as he shoved the screaming woman up and behind him.

As he did this, the balding CPR man reached the dead-looking guy and bent over to give his life saving CPR. Seconds later, he jumped up and gagged after touching his warm, red lips onto cold, blue ones. He was last seen heading toward the bathroom in the next train car.

The woman screamed some more, probably still trying to forget the feel of a dead guy falling on her. Commuters, tired of her screaming, pushed the woman toward the exit door until she was in the other train car. Her screaming continued like in a horror film.

Tony wondered, where the conductors were? Too busy taking the commuter train to the next stop? Must protect the schedule, had recently been the train company's mantra.

The CPR belly man stood over the dead guy and announced to the audience of onlookers, "I touched his skin and he's already gone cold." He rested his hands on his belly, looking puzzled. As if his heroic presence should have justified a resurrection.

Like a heckler, somebody in the audience said, "As fast as the other guy ran, I think he knew CPR wouldn't help, either."

"By the looks of him, he must have been dead and sitting up in his seat for ten minutes or more until he fell over," said the CPR belly man.

"Don't tell that to the woman sitting beside him," said a woman in the back of the crowd.

Everyone decided that watching a dead guy become deader

was spooky. They retreated toward the exits with some deciding to stay. With everyone standing at a distance, Tony faced the dead guy alone. At this moment, he remembered his seatmate.

Tony turned toward the petite man beside him who was of likely Catholic descent since he couldn't stop making the sign of the cross. The Catholic finally broke out of his shock at seeing the dead guy, threw his paperback in the air, and jumped headfirst over the seat in front of him. He scrambled over the next seat headfirst before exiting into the aisle. Tony watched him run out of the train car, never to be seen again.

A quick shift of train tracks relocated the dead guy's torso so that his head and left arm dangled off the seat and into the aisle toward Tony. The remaining commuters receded farther to both ends of the train car, leaving Tony more alone and staring at a rolling head, dangling arm, and questions about why he didn't leave, too.

He wanted to leave, but didn't want to leave the dead guy alone, even if he did take the window seat. For no real reason, Tony thought someone should stay with the body until a conductor showed up. Of all the places to die, Tony felt sorry for the guy dying on a commuter train. He wouldn't want to die on a commuter train. Tony worried that the dead guy might be him one day.

The few commuters remaining at both ends of the train car inched forward. For them, it appeared exciting having a dead guy on a moving train. An Orient Express type of mystery. The remaining commuters looked around to make sure no one else had died.

When the conductors finally arrived from both ends of the train car, Tony took his backpack and moved toward the end of the train car with fewer people. This gave the conductors room to make sure the guy was dead.

For the first time ever, Tony wished he was in his office cubicle already. Usually, the enclosure was like a cage with padded walls where no one heard him living. Yet, now he saw it as his safe place. This realization scared him more than dying on a commuter train.

The conductors told everyone to leave and Tony felt guilty for not helping the would-be CPR heroes. But he also felt guilty for not doing anything to stop this endless commuting. He continued into another train car and did not stop until the last car, which was the quiet car. Everyone was talking about the dead guy. Tony stood in the aisle since there were no empty seats. In the crowd, he spied his office co-worker Debbie talking on her smartphone.

In the past year since they had been riding together, she had yet to notice him even though they worked in the same cubicle farm, albeit at opposite ends. Tony wished he knew her enough to talk about what happened. He thought maybe he should make friends with someone at work or on the train since he spent most of his time at either his job or on the commute. Maybe I should try harder talking to people I see every day, he thought. What was the rest of the day going to bring? And where along the train tracks did the guy die?

It occurred to Tony that maybe the dead guy's soul might not have gotten off. They could be riding a haunted train. It would be hard to sleep on a haunted train. Tony already knew that after chasing the emerald ring ghost, but mostly he wondered why the train kept moving down the tracks.

He guessed they didn't want to make an emergency stop in the middle of nowhere with a man on board who was already dead. It was bad enough having him die on the train unnoticed while everyone read or slept or stared into the back of the seat before them.

Finally, in a series of short pumps, the commuter train eased into the next station. It did not take long for Tony and everyone else to get off. Is death contagious? Sirens and flashing lights mixed with a bright warm sun and a cloudless, blue sky. Tony thought the guy had picked a good day for dying.

Overhead, he saw the news helicopter taking their picture. Some commuters waved. Someone from the train company came with free sugar donuts and coffee. After twenty or forty minutes, two men wheeled a black body bag on a stretcher past them. Most commuters were finishing their second or third helping of donuts. A few raised paper coffee cups to the black bag in a salute of appreciation for the free food and drink.

Tony remembered the dead guy's dark suit and white shirt, as if he dressed for his own funeral. Tony decided he would not wear dark suits and white shirts anymore in case someone thought he was ready to be dead.

People hesitated when the conductors hailed everyone back on the commuter train. Tony thought there should have been some sanctification rites, holy blessing of the train cars to get rid of the guy's ghost. At least a thorough cleansing with formaldehyde for any odor. No to worry, the conductors assured everyone. The train car where the dead guy died had been sealed off. So, could everyone please cram into the other cars like meat packed into tin cans?

Before getting on, Tony saw the woman who did all that screaming sitting in the back of an ambulance with an oxygen mask on. She must have screamed all her air out. Some people huddled around her like the laying of hands, hoping this would help her forget. Tony did not think he would forget a dead man flopping on top of him either. He already had trouble with what he had seen.

On the crowded train, Tony stood in the aisle beside coworker Debbie, who sat in the aisle seat. Maybe it was the experience of death that motivated him to say, "I'm Tony. I work on the same floor with you."

"Oh, hi! I didn't notice you there. Isn't it terrible about Bill? How awful. How are we going to tell people in the office?"

"Bill?"

"Yeah, the guy who died. The one who sits five cubicles over from you at work. It's so terrible that he died like this on a commuter train and on such a beautiful day."

Epilogue

The next day, the local newspaper reported that Bill had a coronary and died before he knew it. Bill's widow planned lawsuits against the commuter train and the freight company who owned the tracks. Tony did not understand what either organization had to do with Bill's death. But he was sure there would be a seat notice requiring people to sign appropriate non-liability forms if they were going to die on the train.

No one moved into Bill's cubicle, maybe because Tony spread the rumor that it was haunted. He wanted the cubicle empty as a shrine to Bill. Apparently, no one else agreed. Eventually, someone rearranged the cubicle to store office supplies, leaving Tony wondering why he did not notice Bill before.

At work, they could have had lunch. What if he had sat beside him on the train that day? No, he would not want a dead man falling on him. All Tony could remember was Bill's dead face.

A month after Bill's death, Tony fell asleep on the evening train home. It was too easy after grabbing a window seat. He figured he'd wake up in time for his stop since he started dreaming right away.

Bill appeared in the seat beside him looking emerald green. Tony wanted to be afraid, or at least concerned that a green ghost sat next to him. But it was a dream and that was okay, he figured.

"You're Bill, but are you also the emerald ring ghost?" Tony asked Bill in the dream.

"No. Your green ghost moved on after that green wine bottle fell off the bridge. I'm this color because he left some residue behind. I'm looking for the place where I died so I can get off this blasted train. Some ghost named Luis is supposed to help me."

Tony watched Bill gradually fade into a sapphire blue. He remained Bill, but only slightly.

"Why are you talking to me in this dream?" asked Tony.

"You're haunted by your wife's death."

"I didn't spend as much time with her as I should have. I was always riding this train. But driving in unpredictable traffic was worse. The only time I spent with Mary was the last few weeks of her life. Can I see her in this dream? Is she on this train?"

"No, she's in the afterlife. I'm only halfway there, like a ghost. But she sent me a message. Both of you had a good time in past lives, and you'll meet again in another life. In the meantime, she wants you to enjoy your daughter and granddaughter. But I have something else to say, too."

"What is it?"

"It's time to wake up."

Tony woke up and felt the train jolt to a stop. He looked out his window to see he was in the train yard. Getting off the train, he remembered Cheryl had quit the train company and wouldn't be giving him a ride. He called Carolyn, who came with Alice and Mary.

"I had a dream about Bill," Tony told Carolyn. Alice and Mary played in the back seat like they were old souls.

"You mean the guy who died beside you on the train? I thought you didn't know him that well," said Carolyn.

"Yeah, that guy. He was on his way to the afterlife. He stopped off in my dream to tell me Mary will meet me in another life."

"Like reincarnation?"

"Yeah, I guess so. In the meantime, it will be the three of us."

"You know, I might find someone one day," said Carolyn. She glanced at her dad for his reaction.

"It's okay. One day I might find someone, too," Tony said with a smile.

Behind them, Alice giggled and Mary looked like she had a smile on her face.

wake up wake up

"Hey, wake up." Angie poked her index finger into the skinny, hard shoulder of the man sitting next to her. They were on the evening commuter train and she did not know how he could sleep with his head back like that and his mouth hanging open. "You have to wake up."

"Why should I wake up?" Annoyed, the man slipped one eye open and half of the other. He left his mouth open.

"You can't sleep next to me, that's why," Angie said.

"Why?"

She wanted to say how she didn't want him dropping dead on top of her like some men did. Yet, she thought that sounded foolish.

"It's like we're sleeping together." After saying this, even Angie thought it sounded even more foolish.

He closed his mouth and sat up, giving her a crooked smile. "We're on a commuter train with lots of people. This is not the same as sleeping together."

Angie pulled her dark blue skirt further over her knobby knees. "Why don't you just stay awake?" She wished she could do something about her knobby knees.

"Why don't you move to another seat if you don't want

me sleeping next to you?"

Angie got off work late and that did not leave her time to travel north and get on the train at the first stop. At least she didn't have to worry about her ex being on the train since he was superstitious about riding the last train in the evening. Angie would ride this train to avoid him, but she didn't like getting home that late every evening.

Besides, this train had too many men with too much body mass. She sat next to this guy because he had the least width. But he was still a man and stubborn as usual. She could be stubborn, too.

"What if you sleep past your stop? I don't know where you get off and I wouldn't wake you up, anyway," said Angie, refusing to move.

"I live alone, so if I sleep past my stop and you're still on the train, you could give me a ride back to my car. By the way, I'm Frank."

Angie didn't like this rationale or that he introduced himself. "No way I'm giving a stranger a ride. You're on your own. You can call your girlfriend or boyfriend."

"Nope, no girlfriend. You're stuck with me."

"Why can't you play video games or watch movies or read like other people on this train? How about that magazine on your lap about acting?" Just seeing the magazine triggered unsettling memories of her father, who also acted.

"You're going to keep me awake talking, aren't you?"

"That's an option," Angie said.

"I get little sleep doing all this commuting to my boring job, which I do it so I can work on my acting. And don't dare suggest I quit the acting. I'd rather quit the boring job and eat peanut butter sandwiches. Why don't you pretend I'm awake with my eyes closed?"

"I don't like actors. My father was an actor. You need to manage your time better and sleep at home." Angie wished she had not said that part about her father. It just came out.

"I manage my time by sleeping on this train. You should accept me as your sleeping partner and let me sleep. We could be bedfellows," said Frank with a smile.

Furious with his comment, Angie grabbed her bag and moved to an aisle seat beside a very wide man. He gave her enough room so she could sit comfortably. I should have sat by him at the start, she thought. Sizeable men like him know how to manage their size. Besides, he stayed awake.

That was the Tuesday evening train. On the Wednesday morning train, Angie woke up with her head hanging forward. She sat in the aisle seat beside some strange man who looked familiar. Hell, they all look familiar, she thought trying to straighten up in her seat while licking the drool from her puffy lips.

She took a deep breath and rubbed a cramp out of her neck from sleeping in an unsleepable position. She wished she had stayed awake because it was too much like sleeping with strangers. The man next to her did not seem to notice as he stirred awake.

Angie looked past him and out the long rectangular train window. She saw the morning sun shining too bright and buildings standing higher than they should. With rising aggravation, she realized her morning stop waited for her one stop back.

"Damn the sea and dry the land," Angie said out of habit. It had been her father's most famous line in an off off off Broadway play, and she treated it like any other cursing. She wished she could remember the name of that play so she could make sure never saw it, if it ever played again.

"This day is already starting out bad," Angie muttered as the commuter train rolled on to another stop. "Now, I've got to take the Metro back to work."

"Sleep past your stop?" The man beside her smiled.

Angie cringed. He was paying her too much attention and his long bushy beard looked fake. Without responding, she got up and queued behind the other commuters. When the train stopped, she followed everyone onto a concrete platform where a gust of wind spun her shoulder length hair across her face, making it hard to see for a moment. Angie nearly fell into the man before her, who had stopped for no other reason than he was a man. A firm hand grabbed her shoulder and gave her back her balance.

Turning around, she saw it was the man with the fake beard. Normally, she liked beards on men because it made them look soft and furry. Except, this man's beard looked itchy. It made her want to scratch her face.

He smiled and walked away, leaving her to put her hair back in place. When done, she lost the direction he went, yet caught the diesel wind from the train engine as it pulled away. The dirtiness pulled at her hair and whipped into her face.

Angie refocused on salvaging her morning. She walked toward the subway, colliding her flats against hard concrete. They had no support and struck a vibrating pain into her legs. They also manufactured a flapping sound, making her think about clowns and their big shoes. Angie wondered if she could survive the rest of her day with a diesel smelling head and floppy shoes.

In the subway waiting for the Metro train, someone behind her said, "How late are you going to be?"

Angie spun around and faced the bearded man. Enough space separated them to stand at least one other person. He's still too near, she thought. "That's none of your business."

Looking at her watch, she realized she would be thirty minutes late for work. She would not tell the stranger. She tried to remember where she'd seen him before that morning.

"Hey, you don't remember me. But yesterday evening you wouldn't let me sleep on the train. I'm Frank."

His grin showed a little of his white teeth through the tangle of dark, wiry hair. At least his teeth are clean, thought Angie. "I think I would've remembered you. In any case, we're not talking anymore." Angie used her best authoritative voice.

"I guess you're grumpy when you first wake up." Frank gave an impish grin.

"This is a big subway. Why don't you go somewhere else?" Standing before him, Angie felt too tall, too short, too thin, and too clumpy.

"The beard! Of course. Hey, I can't take it off, but it's not real. I'm an actor at Riverside Theater near the uptown district. Take a close look. See, it's not real." Frank leaned forward and pulled at the straggly ends of his whiskers.

Angie could see the man's skin pull away as if the bushy beard was glued on.

"It took so long to get it on last night at rehearsal I didn't want to take it off for this morning's run through."

"What play?" Angie was still suspicious, but his eyes seemed familiar.

"*Gregory Thyme through Time.*"

"Never heard of it." On the far wall, she spied a poster that advertised the guy's play. Angie looked closer at the bearded man calling himself Frank.

"Were you on the 5:20 Tuesday evening train?" she asked.

"Yeah, that was me. I was trying to sleep and you—"

"I know. I remember now. You shouldn't have let me fall asleep this morning. You should have stayed awake and kept me awake. I kept you awake that evening."

"I didn't want you keeping me awake that evening. Besides, I'm not sure who went to sleep first this morning. You have a thing about sleeping next to other people, don't you?" said Frank.

Angie refused to admit that she did. It came after falling asleep against her ex a few months ago. He had started sitting next to her on the train and she woke up frightened about losing control beside someone who had hurt her so much.

The subway train arrived with a burst of mechanical air and noise. In the moments they could say nothing, Angie hesitated too long and lost sight of Frank among the commuters who had shifted toward the nearest opened door. She followed the crowd, trying to forget the guy.

Yet, he was an actor that made her think about her actor father and how it had been five years since she last saw him. While on the Metro and trying to forget, she stared at some man's armpit remembering that moment with her father five years ago.

She found him in his dressing room. He was to perform in a Shakespearean play and he always demanded his name be displayed in bold letters on the door. She didn't bother knocking. When she entered, Angie stared at the back of her father's head as he put on his makeup in front of an enormous, lighted mirror.

"What do you want? You know I need this time alone to prepare for my role." Her father switched his focus to the mirror between himself and Angie's reflection. He paid less attention to her reflection and more to the makeup he dabbed on his old face. He tried to make himself look young when he was too old to do so.

"I'm graduating college, which I paid for without your help."

"What degree are you getting?"

"Accounting." Angie immediately wished she had not told him.

In the makeup mirror, he rolled his eyes in a way that said her accomplishment had been a mistake. "Obviously, I can't go to your graduation," he said without feeling. "The show must go on."

"I haven't told you where or when my graduation is. Why don't you admit you were never going?"

"Alright, I'm not going. It's your graduation you paid for."

"I don't know why I'm here. This is all nonsense." Angie felt the mistake of visiting her father like vomit in her throat. Wanting his attention had become too much like begging. Her father turned around since he finished his makeup. Angie thought he looked like a clown.

"I don't know why you're here, either. I have an audience waiting for me. Many people who love my acting."

"And sometimes you loved them back."

"You're aware your mother had her friends over for private parties, too." His voice came out like a sneer.

"I don't care about any of that, now. Why didn't you teach me acting? Why didn't you take an interest in me?"

"I take an interest in what interests me. Sometimes that included you and sometimes not."

"I can't stand this. You've got no talent except with the women you met backstage for your private performances." Angie felt like she was in a shouting match between two people who could not hear.

She looked around and noticed how the lights from the

makeup mirror cast her father's shadow everywhere across the room. Before either of them could say anything more, she spun around and exited the dressing room, no longer believing in her father.

Not long after that talk, Angie's father left for gigs in Asia. He did not attend her college graduation, did not attend her wedding, was not there when she had cancer, nor gave her advice about divorce. Yet, there was one thing Angie despised her father more than anything else. It was leaving behind his wife, her mother, to grow dependent on Angie.

The subway doors opened and Angie pushed her way off, unable to tolerate armpits anymore. She paraded herself between the masses of commuters to climb out of the subway and into better air, where she realized it was the wrong station.

She had another stop to go. Angie promised herself to stop thinking about her father when she was commuting. Now, she would be almost an hour late by the time she got another Metro. People rushed past and she thought about getting back on the subway, except she was not interested in sitting in a cubicle the rest of the day. She called work and took the day off.

With the wind hitting her face and throwing her hair around, Angie stopped in front of a small group of shops that included a cheap-looking salon. She felt impetuous. She expected danger. The beauticians took off extra just to get even at her sharp criticism of their cheap salon.

Riverside Theater was outside the city center, almost in the suburbs, and at the limits of Metrorail in that direction. The last time Angie remembered being there was with her parents, five years ago. Her father was performing some role she did not remember in the Shakespearean play *As You Like It*.

Angie burst into the theater causing the grips to look up at her arrival. The actors on stage, including Frank, tried to ignore her. But she became like them, commanding a presence as she strutted down the aisle with confidence. In the front row, the director stood to face her. He was the director whose name she recognized from the subway poster.

"Damn the sea and dry the land," Angie shouted, approaching the director. Her voice echoed across the theater.

"Who the hell are you?"

"She's with me. A fellow commuter," said Frank from the stage.

She felt drunk with energy as the whole place watched Angie continue down the aisle. At that moment, she controlled this audience of stagehands and actors. Walking up to the director, she did not think her father's famous lines were all that famous.

"I know those lines," said a short, gray-haired, pudgy man who confronted Angie. He portrayed experience that was obvious and successful.

"Years ago, you directed my father in a play. But you knew my mother better."

The director studied Angie until remarking, "I remember now. You're the girl who walked in on us."

"I walked in on my father and his admirers, too. It was something to do," Angie said with a slight smirk.

"Are you going to guilt me into giving you a part in this play?"

"No, what my parents did for recreation was their business. I wrote a one act play about people talking too much on the train. You can use it as an opening for your play. Maybe the critics will go easy on you after seeing what I wrote," said Angie.

The director looked around the stage at things that did not impress him. "I need something other than what I've got. Your mother used to tell me how good a writer you were. Since you're guilting me without admitting it, come back Friday with your play."

The next day, Angie stayed home to work on her play. On Friday morning, she got on the early morning train with a script on her lap. She kept going over in her head what she had to do before opening night in two weeks.

She had become familiar with her tapered short hair and the ability to tolerate Frank who slept beside her. He had no fake beard, but a rash from where one had been. The protagonist in her play did not have a beard.

Running Out of Diesel

Phil's commuter train sat unmoving after running out of diesel twenty minutes from the city on the evening run south. He heard the conductor muttering to himself as he came through, "What a stupid thing the engineer did running out of diesel."

Few people knew that, while the conductor was in charge of the train, the engineer drove it. One had authority to know if the train had enough fuel and the other person had the fuel gauge. The conductor disappeared and Phil hoped he was going for diesel and not an argument with the engineer.

The surrounding lights stayed lit from a battery storage area or some secret Roswell power supply, but nothing else happened. People returned to their reading, sleeping, knitting, gazing at tiny screens, or staring into the back of the seat before them as if they were still click clacking away down the steel rails. Phil worried about the complacency and the inability of the commuters to realize they had become zombies on a never-ending commute.

Everyone sat on the train for thirty-five minutes until a freight train crept past them. The bigger locomotive pulled a long line of open hopper cars filled with foul city garbage and went slow enough to make sure everyone got a good whiff of the strong garbage odor. The fragrance lingered in the commuter train's ventilation system that kept working despite the lack of fuel and movement.

The smell made Phil even more anxious for something to happen and get them moving. He looked around at his fellow commuters who, based on their fidgeting, appeared to be growing anxious, too. Or it could have been the smell making them want to vomit. This latter concern worried Phil because the bathroom was in the next car and they would probably never make it if they needed to use it.

After another ten minutes without the appearance of a conductor or train movement, Phil accepted an invitation from three other commuters to leave the train. The conductors had opened the doors to let out the lingering garbage smell, and this created the opportunity. The opened doors let commuters, who had lost hope, to escape into the descending night air and toward the lights of civilization. Phil figured that if other people were escaping, it must be a good idea.

Of course, the conductors were not authorized to allow this escapism, yet they were outnumbered. As they confronted one group of departurers, another group left from the other door. Phil wondered why the conductors did not simply close the train doors. Maybe they were tired of people complaining and this gave the masses an option to leave, which they were taking.

As the four of them were about to step down the metal stairs onto the tracks, a slim man blocked their way. He carried a derby on his head, a chaotic beard falling off his face, and wore a white shirt with dark khakis and penny loafers without the pennies. Phil had often seen him and nicknamed him Standing Slim because he never sat down. He always stood at some end of a train car until his stop. Now, here he was out of place blocking the exit.

"This is not a stop," said Standing Slim.

"This is no one's stop," the other three men said in unison. They looked at each other, looking pleased with their united answer.

"Why don't you come with us?" Phil had doubts about following these three men who he had never spoken to before.

"I'll wait here. This is expensive equipment to leave sitting around," he said. He stepped out of the way and into the train car, giving Phil a wink.

Phil didn't know what the wink meant. Did Standing Slim know something he should know, too? Phil surveyed the guy's red hair and ruddy complexion as if he had heritage from Scotland or Ireland. Both were countries Phil wanted to visit one day.

He stepped off and saw conductors and engineers arguing near the locomotive. He could not hear them, but the hand gestures said enough. It did not seem diesel fuel was coming anytime soon.

Phil hurried to catch up with his fellow commuters, who headed across the train tracks toward a gravel embankment. Phil had a feeling that he should turn back to look at the unmoving train. He did and caught sight of Angie sitting near a window.

The dim lighting above her seemed to give her face an aura around her face as she leaned back, apparently asleep. He wasn't sure how she could sleep in that position, and he considered going back to sit beside her. Except, one of his fellow excursionists urged him to come along.

Phil remembered the garbage smell, but mostly that he could still make his dinner date with Girlfriend Sheila if he went with these guys. He questioned spending more time with her hormones that sometimes got too loud and critical. He also did not know these men he was following. They were simply the same faces he saw every day riding the rails.

Despite these worries, he followed these men because they invited him along saying three was an odd number to travel with. Phil rarely got invited to anything and he was elated to be included in the social group. Besides, it was better than sitting on a train that had run out of diesel and smelled of trash. Also, Angie was asleep.

Phil followed the three men to the embankment and toward a waiting taxi one of them had called. Phil worried about the cost and why didn't they call a car ride service like an Uber? Based on the people who had already left, he figured taxis were the only option left.

Climbing into the taxi, he sat crammed between two of the wide men and wondered about Standing Slim's wink. Phil considered getting out when the taxi driver sped off as if the police were chasing him.

Before the taxi driver got on the ramp to the interstate filled with barely moving vehicles, they got a flat tire. They all knew it was a flat tire because the right rear drifted and the driver yelled about stupid retreads.

The taxi driver made it into a small parking lot as if this happened to him a lot. Everyone got out to survey a flat rear tire that looked like it would never inflate again. The driver spoke little English, yet they all got the message when he popped open the trunk and held up both palms with an expressive shrug. A quick look proved that the empty tire well should have held something other than stale air and grime.

Phil was not into calamity, but he could taste disaster brewing. One of the other men knew about a bus station he said was, "only a five-minute walk away." They walked twenty minutes to reach it. There they met fellow train commuters already waiting there.

The bus came just when Phil started to leave. No, he did not know where he was going except away from the waiting. He sprinted back and ended up standing in the aisle beside his fellow excursionists, who were seated and ignoring him comfortably. Holding onto an aluminum bar for dear life, he called Girlfriend Sheila on his cell.

"Where are you?"

"I'm on a bus," Phil said, with her needle pitched voice buzzing in his ear.

"How did you get on the bus? I thought you rode the train. Were you telling me the truth about how you get home?"

Phil wondered why they were even together. "I took a taxi from the train, but the taxi got a flat."

"What about the train?"

He did not want to tell her since she worked for the train company. If they knew he knew the train ran out of diesel, he could be banished from riding back and forth to places he did not want to be for knowing the train ran out of diesel. An embarrassment to the train company. Phil realized Girlfriend Sheila was chattering away at him.

"Sorry, the line broke up." That always worked with people who talked too much.

"I said, where are you headed?"

"To the commuter bus lot. Can you pick me up there?" Phil tried not to sound desperate. He hated asking her for anything since she complained for days.

"You found a way from the train to a bus. You can find a way home."

He did not know whether Sheila pushed the end button or he lost the signal. He always thought the road to love meant doing things for each other. Obviously, only Phil had that perception of their relationship. It did not matter since he smelled an obnoxious fume mixed with the sound of metal shavings being born from somewhere below their feet.

It was just before the ramp to the interstate with stop and go traffic when the bus turned down a narrow road. That was where it shuddered to a stop, like a dying breath. The small meek-looking driver stood up slowly and faced his passengers, who anticipated helpful options for alternative transportation. Instead, the bus driver erupted in a stream of broken English, blaming everyone for breaking down his bus.

He continued blaming everyone for how he made more money in this country than his own. He ended with ranting that lapsed into his native language and sounded like a string of curses. Phil hoped curses did not work if the cursed person did not understand the curserer.

"Get off my bus."

They all understood those words.

The neighborhood they exited into smelled like the trash train. Someone said something and they all turned around to spot their commuter train sitting on the train tracks less than a hundred yards away. Yes, they had gone in a circle.

The train doors remained opened as the group of impatient commuters trudged back toward the train. Phil noticed Angie was no longer at the window. He and the wayward flock presented their exposed selves to the audience of passengers who had stayed and did not care about them. In all this time, Phil still did not have a meaningful conversation with any of his three fellow excursionists. On board the commuter train, he went left and they went right.

"I'm back on the train," Phil told Girlfriend Sheila on his cell.

"I called my office and your train broke down," she said.

Phil tried to act very excited about this revealing piece of obvious news. "Are they sending help?"

"Oh, I don't know. I thought you said you were in a taxi and then a bus. Are you still hungry? I am."

"No, not anymore." It would not do any good being hungry since the train did not include a café car.

"Since you'll be late, I'm going to get something to eat with my friends."

My friends irked Phil. He thought Sheila should have used her influence with the train company to get them some help.

"Did your office say what they're doing to get us going?" Phil asked into a dead phone.

He took a deep breath, breathed a heavy sigh, and wished smartphones had not been invented. Looking for news about moving the train, Phil stepped outside and stumbled into a hazy bloom of smokers. Fading emergency lights from the rectangular windows faded down on them.

"What's happening with getting us moving again?" Phil's question sent a half dozen eyes rolling and he guessed the situation had already been discussed ad nauseam among this private death club.

"They've got an engine coming to push us down the road," the conductor said with a cigarette in his mouth that flipped ashes into the dark as he talked.

"Can't the next scheduled train pick us up?"

"Already did. Got as many on as it could. Everyone still here had either wandered off and came back or didn't want to stand on a crowded train."

Phil pictured a bunch of nicotine sufferers who had nothing to go home to all clumped together outside a commuter train that was going nowhere.

"How much longer before the engine shows up?"

"'Bout twenty minutes."

Phil didn't bother looking for Angie. He figured she got on the other train. He sat inside and called Girlfriend Sheila.

"Hey, where are you?" Phil asked. In the background, he heard loud laughter.

"A bar with my friends. Stop it, Tommy." Giggling burst into Phil's ear. "Hey, we'll catch up with each other later this week," she said. Before ending the call, Phil caught a deep baritone voice pleading for her attention.

It would be easy to tell Sheila over the phone tomorrow that they were finished. I could end the call before she laughed at me because she never considered us a couple who needed breaking up, he thought.

Phil leaned back against his seat listening to the silence. The emergency lighting dimmed, and this rare stillness bid him to appreciate it. Far off, he heard the city move, but he let those noises drift away.

He slipped into a state of calmness as the emergency lights faded to nothing, allowing the inside to equal the outside for darkness. In the distance through the wide windows, he saw the city lights gave off a bloom into brightness. Phil saw through his window the broken bus sitting like a grave marker. Sad to think a commuter train felt like home, Phil thought. He turned around to see who was coming down the aisle.

Standing Slim stood beside Phil and pulled out two small bottles of wine from his backpack. He handed Phil a merlot and kept a chardonnay for himself. They drank in silence as the tall man stood looking up and down the train car like trying to find someone not there.

"All we can hope for is that everything we experience becomes a picture to remember," Standing Slim said as he took a long swallow of his wine.

"What are you talking about?"

"I stayed on the train because eventually it will have to be moved since it's in the way of more important freight trains."

"It's sitting off a spur and out of the way," Phil said.

Standing Slim looked at Phil as if there was nothing wrong with the situation. "Do you know why I never sit down?"

Phil didn't care as long as Standing Slim did not make the train late.

"I like people noticing me. No one notices me at home. I only know my wife and daughters through their social media sites. They all have friends to socialize with while I have no social strength to connect with them. I'm happy on the train with people around. The train tracks sing to me when I need it."

Phil tried to sympathize. "During the short days of winter, I ride the train in the dark both ways. Sometimes, I look out the window and have to think hard about whether I'm going to work or coming home. Really, I just hope I don't sleep past my stop again." He finished his wine, realizing he failed to sympathize.

Finishing his wine and taking Phil's empty bottle toward the trash can, Standing Slim called back, "You should have stayed on the train and sat with Angie."

He kept walking into the next train car. Phil thought he was coming back, but he did not. Phil wanted to ask Slim how he knew about Angie. He leaned back in his seat and closed his eyes wishing he had more wine. Their brief talk hurt his tired brain, but made him feel something. He wondered when that train engine was coming to push them home.

It came just then with a loud bang.

The train car shuddered in nervous suddenness as another bang plunged the train forward as if planning to bump them all the way home. A group of passengers behind Phil let out a loud squeal of laughter, sounding like fingernails across a blackboard. A typical cliché because Phil could think of nothing else in this unhappy, unsettled, and unquiet moment of his life.

The wild bumping stopped as the train's neon lights exploded with brightness. Blinded temporarily, Phil stopped clenching the back of the seat before him as the commuter train unfolded into a consistent movement forward.

Forty-five minutes later, Phil got off the train. Yet, he did not go home, but went to a café near the train station opened for people not wanting to go home. He had a beer with his fried fish sandwich and did not talk to the other solitary commuters who also ate the special alone.

The next day, Sheila called Phil to say she got fired because the train ran out of diesel. "It wasn't my fault," she said. "Tommy picked me up at the office early and I forgot to process the paperwork. They should have had someone backing me up. You were on that train and a long-time rider. They might listen to you. Why don't you tell my boss to give me a second chance?"

Phil ended the call and blocked her phone number.

That evening, Phil found Standing Slim standing at the end of a train car. Enough stops had been stopped to leave empty seats nearby. Phil sat down in one and offered Slim a small bottle of white wine.

"Sorry, but I forgot what kind of white you liked."

"I like all free wine."

Phil slurped his red wine before asking, "You ever talk to anyone on the train?"

"I talked to you yesterday."

"Besides me that one time."

"People don't talk to someone standing up while they're sitting."

"Maybe it strains their neck to look up?"

"Maybe. But people are prejudiced about anyone different." Standing Slim finished his wine without slurping and handed the empty to Phil. "Sometimes I enjoy being alone and being different is a lot better than being the same."

Standing Slim got off at the next stop. Phil after that at the last stop. Angie also got off with Phil, but she moved fast like she was late for an appointment.

Clyde is as Big as a Hero

Standing on the train station platform, Clyde felt the chilly air gather around him as the sun sank behind the city buildings. Before him were empty tracks and behind him a crowd of impatient commuters waiting for a train that was ten minutes late.

The lateness caused murmurs of anxiety to ripple through the crowd, who wanted to get on with the commute and out of the descending cold and darkness. Clyde glanced to his right at a thinnish woman standing no taller than his shoulders. He noticed her even though he tried not to. He was a very fat man standing next to a smallish woman and the contrast made him feel even fatter.

He remembered her that one time in the parking lot after his bathroom incident when he had to rush home and pee. He thought of telling her his bathroom story now, yet he could feel the tenseness in her.

He watched her stare past him toward a bend in the tracks where the train should be coming. Her tense jaw and squinting eyes showed her trying to will the train to come. She glanced up at Clyde, maybe wanting him to use his will power, too. Clyde looked at her looking at him and he looked away. She made him nervous with those squinting brown eyes.

"You're bigger than everyone here," she said, turning toward the empty tracks. Puffs of her breath punched the chilly air in front of her.

"What do you mean by that?" Clyde's aggravation rose, thinking she meant he was the fattest person in the crowd. He wanted her to admit it.

"You're significant in this crowd. They can't intimidate you. They can't bully you around. No one can even see me." She stared at the train tracks as if she was frozen in place.

"I don't want to talk about our body sizes. I'm sorry." Clyde wished he had not apologized. He sounded like he was apologizing for his size or hers. He wished he had explained how being fat was much more than overeating. There was mother, father, and childhood issues. If he explained this, they would stand there for hours in the cold, which would bring on hypothermia long before he finished.

They both stood in the cold and faced the empty train tracks. Clyde forgot about the woman and thought about his position on the platform. He smiled. He had arrived at the station early enough to stand in this prime spot where the train doors usually opened. Clyde enjoyed that his size commanded this place on the platform. He would be the first on the train car with his option of available seats. He couldn't help but glance again at the smallish woman beside him.

She used to stand near the back of the crowd, but lately he saw her already on the train after getting on at an earlier stop. This evening she arrived early, the same as him, and he wondered if she was still trying to get away from her ex-husband.

Clyde couldn't sleep on the train, so he paid attention to his fellow commuters. He caught glimpses of talks she had with a man who sometimes sat beside her: her ex who wanted to get back together. Clyde was glad it was not working. He liked her and he did not like him.

Maybe I should say something to her about the weather or how people, even fat people, enjoyed standing near me. It made them look smaller. Before he could say anything, either the darkening sky, coldness of the air, or continued lateness of the train hit some unmentioned threshold among the crowd behind them. Muttering began and it grew in volume as the waiting commuters tense up. He glanced behind him. At the back of the crowd, people had arrived for the next train.

These commuters, like him, who arrived early to nab the best spot on the platform. These other commuters added their fleshy mass to the volume of people wanting to go home. Or at least get out of the cold.

Saying nothing, the small woman next to Clyde tried to back away from the train tracks. She got half a step before bumping into two tall, pudgy men who did not move because they could not or just didn't want to. With an exasperated sigh, the short woman twisted around and faced them. Yet, they continued to look over her head for a train that refused to come.

Clyde noticed how she pressed her bony arms tight against her sides. She appeared to be trying to keep warm, suppress a rising panic, or fly off like Rocket Woman. He regretted ending their conversation and, before he could decide on something to say, they all heard the distant rumble of the train's approach.

Everyone swung their heads toward the bend in the tracks where the toot toot of a small horn confirmed the coming of the commuter train. Thinking it would make the train come faster, the waiting commuters took a step forward.

Excited that he could be first on the train with his choice of seats, Clyde stood his ground and forgot about the woman beside him. All he could think about was how he wouldn't have to sit with people grimacing when he sat next to them. If they sat beside him, it would be their fault.

"Excuse me," she said, still facing the crowd.

Her words were misunderstood, not heard because of her quiet voice, or ignored by the impatient commuters. Clyde thought someone besides himself should have noticed that she faced the wrong way to board a commuter train.

A shift in the wind and Clyde caught the sweet fragrance of her perfume, moody in a nice sort of acidity way. It had the taste of her anxiety coming out slowly, cautiously. The same as a thermonuclear explosion.

"Don't worry," Clyde told her. "They won't push you on the train tracks because that would make the train even later." It was a bad joke he realized that only increased the look of rising panic in the small woman. She ignored him while the other commuters ignored her.

The commuter train came around the bend and headed the short distance to their station. Everyone kept staring as if the train might disappear if they looked away. Clyde looked down at the woman who continued facing the wrong way. She looked focused on panic and escape. Maybe not in that order.

She held up her open palms toward the two men in front of her and tried to move past them without touching. This was impossible. She could not compete with the quantity of human flesh massed together and staged for entry into an approaching train car. A slight tremble erupted from her voice.

"Excuse me," she said to anyone listening.

No one was listening. The impatient commuters ignored

her tiny noise as the thunderous train engine approached. Commuters looked over her head, watching to see where the doors would open, like watching the ball on a roulette table. The best she could do was face armpits and bellies.

"Can't you wait another minute for the train to get here?" Clyde shouted above the coming noise of the train engine. "The doors will open almost where we're standing and I'll let you in front of me," he pleaded.

A diesel engine came and crushed a barrier of dirty wind through the crowd who seemed to explode with the anticipation of getting out of the cold. The quieter, rattling noise of the train cars came next as the moving structures struggled to a stop. The short woman appeared not to have heard Clyde. He saw panic in her eyes. Clyde understood panic. He panicked almost every morning that his previous day's weight gain would confine him to bed forever.

"I can't wait," she said in a weak, strained voice.

"All right, I'll get you out of here." Clyde faced the worried crowd because he was bigger than all of them, at least in width. "Follow me," he said as he stepped between her and the crowd of commuters.

"Excuse me, people. I need to get this lady out of the crowd." At least my size is good for something, he thought.

An opening appeared in the crowd. Proudly, he kept his back straight as much as he could and led the small woman through the mass of commuters. He wondered how the people found the room to let him through until he realized they filled in the large space he left behind. The mass of people slid around him like he was a glob of oil moving through water.

Clyde passed through the human mass before realizing it. He stood next to her at the back of the crowd and watching people funnel into the stopped train car.

"I'm alright, now," she said, and hurried away.

"Wait."

She walked fast, slapping her flats onto the concrete platform and making the sound of flippers. Clyde turned toward the train and saw that the doors had opened exactly where he had been standing. He would have been first on the commuter train. Now, behind the crowd, he would be last and would probably have to stand.

He became infuriated with the woman. "She never even thanked me. She walked away from me like I wasn't even here. How can she dismiss my size so easily? I am not this big for nothing." Talking loudly to himself, Clyde's hot breath hung in the chilly air and drifted back into his face.

He glared at her, walking swiftly to the first train car next to the engine where she disappeared up the metal steps. She walked away from me like I was some hideous monster, he thought.

Clyde pushed his large body toward the door where the woman had gone and he got there long after she and the other commuters had disappeared inside. He grabbed the metal handrails to pull himself up in a battle against gravity. The handrails were cold from people not needing them.

In the cavity of the train car, he spied her nestled alone at the far end closest to where it connected to the engine. Seats were available because this was the quiet car that most commuters avoided. People did not appreciate conductors and self-appointed commuters telling them to be quiet. Instead, they crowded into the other cars, listening to their electronic devices with headphones and not saying anything to anyone. The quiet car was also so close to the engine that the noise prevented anyone from hearing anything.

Clyde pushed his bulk down the narrow aisle, sidestepping

past the back of the seats that held the aisle to an aisle form. He did not care that people leaned out of his way when he fleshed past them.

Anyone watching could see that Clyde's mass could not easily slip into the compact seat next to this thin woman without pushing something aside. He didn't care and lowered his body fat down, feeling his ass push outward as pressure from his upper body met the seat's strong resistance.

"I've given you some more room, mister," she said in a child's whisper.

Clyde looked down and realized she was right. She had angled herself into the corner of her seat, exposing a smidgen more of precious seat space.

"I don't know how I got out of that crowd back there. I think I forgot to thank you for helping me." Her whispering made a gentle wind.

"You seemed to be panicking." Clyde did not care that he spoke a little too loud to be quiet. The train had not started moving, and he figured the quietness did not start until movement arrived and the engine roared to life.

"I don't know what came over me. Maybe I got too cold. I'm sorry you lost your place in line."

"It doesn't matter. This seat is just as good." Sitting beside her was better than sitting beside someone who resented his size, Clyde thought.

"I'm Angie. Thanks for your help. I should have thanked you before, but I wanted to get inside and calm down," she said while pulling out an e-reader.

The engine groaned to life, bringing a loudness echoing throughout the quiet car. While it built rumbling momentum pulling away from the station, Clyde disappeared from Angie's attention. It was time to be quiet amid all the noise. It was hard to have a conversation, anyway.

The train went across steel tracks with the two of them riding silently in the quiet car. At the stops, he tried to think of something to say before the train moved again. Yet, his mind was in confusion as he sat there smelling her sweet perfume.

At a train stop, she queued up and got off with other passengers, big and small. He used to get off at that train stop and suddenly remembered when he got stuck in the bathroom. The story he should have told her. The one they could have laughed about and maybe gone out to dinner after. Instead, the train carried him away from her.

Watching her walk away was when he realized he hadn't introduced himself. She didn't know who I am, Clyde thought. He considered running after her, but grinned at the image of himself lumbering off the train yelling his name like it would save them all from the commute. No one can be saved.

Maybe tomorrow evening I'll get the chance to introduce myself and tell her my funny bathroom story. I'll find her in the crowd, even if I have to give up my good spot again on the station platform.

Riding to his stop, Clyde thought about trying another diet before saying anything to Angie. Getting off, his stomach hurt and he dispensed any will power that remained to control his appetite.

He sighed with heaviness as he drove home, where he would cook a pound of buttered pasta. However, at his apartment he thought about Angie and how they could be train partners if he didn't get too much bigger. He could somehow help her avoid her ex.

Thinking about her brought back some of his will power. At least enough that he only cooked half a pound of pasta, added more butter, but left off the parmesan.

Sudden Stops

The conductor burst into the train car and plopped down in the first train seat he could find.

"Just stay where you are, please," he called out over the sounds of thumping under the train car. The commuter train attempted to make a sudden stop as the steel wheels shook, rattled, and squealed on the steel rails.

"The emergency exit is by me." Phil cringed at his high-pitched tone. It sounded panicky and he wished he had kept quiet. Yet, the train's squealing and rattling drove up his anxiety. The commuter train took a long time trying to stop quickly.

Again, he looked up and read the "Emergency Evacuation" sticker on the window beside him. It explained how the thirty-pound glass could be easily removed by pulling on the red handles at either end. Designed to fall inward, it would hit his head causing minor bone fractures. He imagined becoming a springboard for the melee of panicked passengers trampling over him to get out.

He was glad only two people were in this train car. One person sat near the front and the other stood at the rear. They would create a melee he could easily avoid. It was only them on this last Friday evening train since most people rode the earlier trains to get the weekend started as soon as possible. Also, there was only one stop left. Phil rode this train because going home to a small apartment left him no reason to get there any earlier.

The commuter train finally stopped with one bumpy jerk. Seconds later, the fluorescent lights turned off and the air blower ceased. Emergency lighting and descending quiet filled in for the lack of motion. Phil wondered how long it would take for the outside cold to filter in.

He watched the conductor get up and walk through the exit door, heading into the next train car without explaining why there had been a sudden stop. Phil sat in the middle of the train car and considered following him, but he didn't want to leave his emergency window. At least not yet.

Phil surveyed his two fellow commuters. He had traveled with them countless times before and still did not know their actual names. So, he nicknamed them Don't Jump Ben and Always Falling Asleep Sue for no other reason than he saw them every day on the commute and wanted to call them something. Nicknaming his fellow commuters helped keep him from worrying he could die one day in a train wreck with a bunch of strangers.

Don't Jump Ben stood in the train's rear looking out the window that was the top half of the door. This was the last train car with nothing behind them and he could see what the train had passed over such as the steel rails, stone gravel, and creosote beams that made up the train tracks. He could also jump off the train if the locked door swung open, or he pushed his window out like it was designed to do in an emergency.

Always Falling Asleep Sue always took the first seat available as she got on the train and immediately went to sleep. Now, with the conductor gone, Phil watched her wake up, flopping her mass of curly brown hair around.

"Don't bother waking up. Might be a long delay," announced Don't Jump Ben. His gravelly voice belched from the pregnant roundness of his belly and jumped across the empty seats.

Always Falling Asleep Sue turned around in her seat and stretched her legs across the aisle. "I can't sleep. It's too quiet."

These were the first words Phil ever heard either of them say. He wanted to be part of the conversation and said, "I wish the conductor had told us why were stopped so suddenly." He did not say how grateful he was they were still on the rails and not turned over or sitting in a place that had no rails.

"At least you're safe next to the emergency exit," Sue said with a grin.

Phil could not reply. He was shocked she had heard him.

Ben said, "I like this quiet and being stuck here. I don't have to put up with whatever's at either end."

Sue said, "I can see the conductors outside with their flashlights. They're looking under the train cars."

"That thumping could have been a body," said Ben. "That would keep us here awhile."

"I hate it when the train is delayed like this. I'd rather be doing almost anything than riding this train," Sue said. "I wouldn't be here if my divorce hadn't forced me into a full-time job so far from home."

Sitting in the middle of the train car, Phil sat sideways, looking back and forth between the two. He wanted to think of something to say and join the conversation. He watched

Sue look at her watch, at her nails, then out the darkened window across from her. Finally, she pulled out her smartphone. This took up almost a minute.

"It's been four minutes since we stopped," she announced, almost to herself.

"I wish someone would tell us what's going on," said Phil.

"Maybe we have stopped existing. That would be alright with me. It would make this commute more interesting and like an adventure," said Ben.

Phil worried about the eerie quiet descending on them, as if sound ceased to exist. He also worried that he was becoming dependent on sitting next to the emergency window in case there was an emergency. There was never an emergency, just train delays like this one.

"I don't need an adventure," said Sue. "I've had enough adventures lately."

"Yeah, what adventure could you have had?" A smirk spread across Ben's face.

While thumbing through her smartphone, Sue said, "I'm only riding this train after I told my ex about my affair with a cowboy. Instead of being thankful I told him, he divorced me and moved into the city where he doesn't have to commute anymore. He left me riding this stupid train."

Ben snickered. "A cowboy? Yeah, I bet that was an adventure." He left the smirk hanging between them as he turned to look out his darkened window.

Neither said anything in a kind of stand-off. Ben stared out the darkened window and Phil wondered what he was looking at with the train not moving. Maybe the conductors?

"What are you looking at?" Phil asked.

"I'm looking at some pictures of my niece. You want to see?" Sue walked toward Phil's seat and plopped down next to him.

Phil panicked. Should he tell her he was talking to Ben and not her? Neither knew who Ben was. Phil caught a whiff of Sue's fragrance, smelling sweet and musty. The odor disappeared among the sweaty stench of former commuters who got off at other train stations and were home by now. She thrust the face of her phone toward him.

He found himself staring at a snapshot of a smiling baby in the lap of a thick man. Was the baby happy about the wet spot she created on the man's pants? Sue showed Phil only this one picture before taking the phone away.

"Nice. Your brother's or sister's?" This was the best Phil could do. He never understood people's excitement with baby pictures.

"My younger sister's child. They live on the west coast."

"I don't have children. If I ever stop commuting, I plan on getting a dog," Phil said. Sue seemed to make him say awkward things.

"I'd be afraid a dog would want too much from me. I'm more of a people person." She stayed in her new seat looking at more pictures on her smartphone. Ones she did not show Phil.

He stared into the back of the seat in front of him, feeling the nearness of Sue's body. Just as he thought of something to say, Angie walked past them and stepped into the bathroom across from Ben.

"We might be here awhile. I think I'll finish my nap," said Always Falling Asleep Sue. She slouched in her seat next to Phil and closed her eyes.

Phil desperately wanted Sue to go away before Angie came back. It's going to look like I have something going on with this woman sleeping next to me when there are all these empty seats nearby, he worried. He tried to think of something to say and get Sue back to her seat when Ben spoke up.

"My girlfriend looks great when she's sleeping. She's not nagging me or eating too much."

"So what if she gains a little weight? You gonna dump her?" Sue popped open her eyes.

"All I'm saying is my girlfriend looks good because I keep on her about her weight."

Sue sat up and focused on Ben like she wanted to wish him through the door and onto the train tracks. "So, if she gained weight or did something else you didn't approve of, you'd dump her?"

"Damn right. Why keep her? Too many women would like to have a piece of me."

"A piece of you is right." Sue could not finish because Angie came out of the bathroom diverting all their attention.

Phil did a poor job of averting his eyes as she went by, realizing the opportunity to have her sit beside him had vanished. Ben kept his eyes on Angie until she was out the exit door.

Sue said, "I hope she doesn't come back. I'm not getting much sleep with all this staring. Also, why are you always looking out the back window?" Sue asked Ben. She sounded like she wanted a confrontation.

"I'm holed up in a cubicle all day and I enjoy watching the scenery go by. This is my corner of the universe. I deserve this."

"I guess we all deserve something," Sue said with a smirk, much like Ben's.

"I sit a lot at my job, too. I'm working on a project everyone is hot about." Phil wondered if he should stop trying to be a part of the conversation.

"Okay, you have an important job. What's your project

about?" Sarcasm washed through Ben's voice.

"My team is trying to find a statistical correlation between the manufacture of burial caskets and the making of hardwood floor coverings."

"What the hell for?" asked Sue.

Phil realized he had fallen off some imaginary cliff and had no choice but to finish falling. "Because one of my bosses saw the two terms next to each other on a data sheet of miscellaneous items."

Don't Jump Ben gave a snorting type of laugh. Always Falling Asleep Sue had a sniffling type of giggle. Both ended in a brief, full-blown laugh. Phil had no hope that his comment would be forgotten.

"Yeah, you're a federal worker," Ben said.

"Only the government would think of a project like that and call it important," said Sue. Still amused, she got up and went back to her seat at the front of the train car.

Phil faced the back of the seat, terrified about what had happened. I should never have tried talking to these people, he thought. He was aggravated. Why do I care about them, anyway? I'm better off at home with my fish who blurp at me with soundless bubbles, Phil concluded. He wondered when the train would start moving. He didn't want to spend any more time with these two. I'll go look for Angie and maybe sit by her, he decided. He didn't get a chance.

A vomit of noise erupted from every point of the train car. The three of them grabbed something to hold on to as neon lights sprayed them with brightness and manufactured air rushed into the car. With a heavy jolt, the commuter train thrust itself forward.

A few minutes later, the missing conductor appeared from where other train cars existed.

"We hit a deer and part of it got caught underneath the train cars. You might have heard it thumping around under your feet. But, no worry. No damage."

The conductor gave a toothy grin with some teeth missing and disappeared into the vestibule.

"I hope the deer didn't tear something we'd need later like brake hoses." Now that they were moving, Phil hoped they could stop.

"I'm sure we'll be fine," said Sue, smiling. "Besides, you're safe next to that emergency window."

Embarrassed, Phil picked up his backpack from between his feet and plopped it in the seat vacated by Always Falling Asleep Sue. It was heavy, not from the creative writing magazine with too many advertisements, an electronic device that needed recharging, or office work he probably would not work on that weekend, but the copy of the novel he was writing.

Phil could not figure out why he carried it on his commute every day. He looked at the emergency window, realizing he could be thrown into it and knocked unconscious in a derailment. Then his backpack with his novel could be lost.

This is ridiculous, he thought. My novel would not be lost, just left unread and unwanted like he had become sitting on a commuter train every day. Phil thought about how Ben and Sue had laughed at him. He had to admit the project was stupid. He should have laughed with them.

This is what I'll do, he decided. I'll tell Sue about the nickname I have for her and Don't Jump Ben. She might find that funny. I'll redeem myself that way. Phil grabbed his backpack, determined to ask Always Falling Asleep Sue's what her name was.

Except, Don't Jump Ben had slipped past him to sit next

to her in the front seat. Phil went to a seat behind them.

As the train slowed for the last station, he heard Ben and Sue talk about meeting at the Ruby Tuesday bar when they got off. Sue introduced herself as Claudia, but Phil missed Ben's actual name. It didn't matter, he thought.

They made confrontational, sarcastic remarks to each other and laughed. They were not people he would talk to again. Phil stood and queued in front of the exit door, wondering if one person made a queue.

Like all exit doors, the upper half was a window. Through it he peered into the vestibule where the train cars connected. On the other side, through the half door window, he spotted Angie who had queued up, too. She was staring at him.

He and she became the only two people queued up. We're in this together, thought Phil. If the train derailed at this moment, we would either be the first ones off or the first to die. Phil wanted to tell her this or something not as ridiculous. He pushed a panel that triggered the pocket door to slide open. A rush of metallic noise struck his face, coming from basic functions of where the train cars connected.

By opening the door, Phil now saw the conductor standing on his side of the vestibule. The conductor was waiting for the train to stop so he could push the buttons and open the outside doors. Angie had been staring at the conductor, anticipating the moment of the push. The conductor stared at Phil for breaking the rules and opening the vestibule door. Phil stared at Angie, who continued staring at the conductor. All this staring made Phil uneasy.

So close to the station, the conductor said nothing to Phil as the train bumped to a stop. The cessation of train movement and noise gave way to exiting commuters making a fuss with their complicated handling of bags, backpacks, and satchels.

Angie was quick off the train. Phil wondered why she was in such a hurry. Did it have something to do with Paula's group he heard about? On the station platform, the contents of his backpack spilled out. He forgot to zip it up.

After repacking his backpack, Phil charged up the platform stairs, intending to catch up with Angie in the parking lot. When he got to the top, she was already getting in her car. She led the other commuters out of the parking lot.

Standing beside his car, Phil wanted an adventure instead of riding the train back and forth every day. But not an adventure like Claudia or what Ben imagined. His adventure would be leaving his emergency exit window. Maybe to go looking for Angie and ask her how her play was coming along.

Clyde's Hunger

The short toot toot of a train horn echoed through the tall city buildings, urging Clyde to walk faster. He was less than a block away from the station and he wanted to be on the arriving commuter train.

There was no reason for him to be on *that* train. He had come early to be on the next one so he could get a good spot on the platform, be first on the train, and have his choice of train seats. Yet this approaching train was late enough that, if he made it, he could get home a little earlier.

Then what, he asked himself? So, I have more time to eat and get fatter? Besides, I'll be one of the last on this train and may not even get a seat. Yet, Clyde could not convince himself to do anything but give in to his competitive urges and pick up his pace.

It was an anxious decision that brought on indigestion erupting into his throat along with a sharp pain driving into his arthritic left knee. He kept going anyway through the heat, thick humidity, and of course the pain.

He tried to forget about his knee, which caused him to blunder into a memory of when he was eleven-years-old. It was Thanksgiving morning at breakfast and his thin father had barely eaten anything. He leaned across the table and said into Clyde's face, "Thanksgiving is a useless holiday making people weak with all that excess food. Don't be a loser and let food take over your life."

Father was wrong. Clyde had long ago decided he was stronger when he ate. It was getting fat that made me struggle to get to the train just now, he thought. Sweating and out of breath, Clyde reached the end of the block. Across the street he saw the long walkway leading to the commuter train sitting with its doors opened like hands welcoming him onboard. Taking a moment to catch his breath, Clyde knew he had made it. Yet, when he stepped into the street, the neon sign with the happy green walking man transformed into a menacing red hand demanding him to stop.

Like bursting out of a starting gate, rush hour traffic whizzed past him. Across the street, he glared at the last of the commuters funneling onto the train. I need to be on that train, he demanded of himself. With growing agitation, he stepped further onto the street's hot, black tar.

Inching out, no vehicle would stop for him. Don't they realize how much damage my size will cause to their vehicles? Clyde picked his way in front of newer, expensive cars, hoping the drivers would be more cautious. They scowled at him and dared him to cross their path. They were probably rich enough to buy new, expensive cars.

Was it worth risking injury to be on this train and get home earlier? Clyde didn't care. If his father was alive and in this situation, the risk would have been worth it. Behind Clyde, the commuters waiting to cross the street yelled at him to stop.

He ignored them and inched across the street as heartburn filled his chest and his knee throbbed in pain. Halfway across the road, he dashed for the walkway, too obsessed with making the train to worry about a vehicle hitting him. With heavy breathing, Clyde stumbled across the curb and was so satisfied that he made it he wanted to laugh. He glanced back at the other commuters behind him.

They were now crossing the street. The happy green man on the pole looked like he was laughing at Clyde. With his breath laboring against his body's excessive bulk and his heart pounding furiously, Clyde just knew those people wouldn't make it. They're too far away. But I'll make it. I'll win.

He lumbered toward the open train door, ignoring the conductor waving her palms to slow him down. Out of breath and sweating badly, Clyde got to the door and looked toward the other end of the train he could not see before.

A woman in a wheelchair was just being lifted into a train car. It would be another five minutes before the train moved. Clyde stood there struggling to catch his breath, and he glowered at the other commuters crossing the street toward him. He wished they would get stuck on the hot tar.

"Hey, I tried to tell you back there the light was changing," said a pudgy man carrying his suit coat across his left arm. His shirt lacked any patches of sweat. He stepped up into the doorway of the idling train car as if Clyde never existed.

The conductor let another four passengers get on the train. They were all the people Clyde left waiting at the light. He felt aggravated at being put in this embarrassing situation. When the train was ready to leave, he stood in the open doorway preventing the conductor from closing the metal doors.

Clyde savored this time, knowing he held the commuter train hostage by his lack of movement and size. It was his moment. His revenge for those five people who should be waiting for the next train. The conductor gave Clyde a hostile stare like she would ban him from riding the train forever if he didn't move. This convinced Clyde to climb inside. He hated driving in rush hour traffic.

The five commuters to get on took the last available seats. All Clyde could do was shove his way down the narrow aisle, ignoring people leaning away from his sweaty bulk. He hunted for a cool air vent to stand under.

He found it in front of the door leading into the next train car. In this spot, a draft of cool, manufactured wind convinced him it was the best he could do. Clyde leaned against a maintenance panel, letting his sweat evaporate and not feeling any better.

He wished the indigestion boiling in his gut would boil away and stop trying to escape through his throat. *If I could eat something, I might feel better.* Except, the commuter train got rid of the café car to transport more commuters. The train had style back then, Clyde remembered.

He switched position, taking weight off his aching knee and hoping his other knee could hold up. Yet, a sudden switch of tracks shoved him one way and then the other. Searching for balance, Clyde stepped with his bad knee, causing throbbing pain to rip up his leg like a dull knife cutting into his bone. Closing his eyes and grimacing, he propelled into the memory of when he first hurt his knee.

This memory shoved its way on him like a persistent sadness from his childhood. He continued to be that skinny eleven-year-old on Thanksgiving Day. This time it was early afternoon at the kitchen table. He sat watching his mother at a nearby counter open pre-packaged food delivered by a caterer. His father stood across the table, refusing to sit down and scowling at his wife.

"All I'm asking is that we have this one meal together. I

need to tell people we had a proper Thanksgiving dinner. It's embarrassing when I have to make up something to tell people every year," Mother told Father.

The meal was part of her manipulation of society gossip rather than any attempt at family unity. It did not matter to Clyde, nor did he care his father refused to let relatives attend. This would be the feast everyone talked about in school. His mother wore the proud expression that she would be a somebody in the town's society circles.

"And I'm telling you I don't have time for this nonsense. I need to finish my business plan for an executive meeting tomorrow." Clyde's father stepped forward and used his body to block his short wife from bringing more food to the table.

"Clyde needs a Thanksgiving meal so I can explain to the golf club tomorrow how well we treat our ungrateful son." She deftly maneuvered around her husband, carrying a heavy-looking bowl of mashed potatoes. It was enough for the entire neighborhood.

"Look at how pitiful and weak my son is just waiting to eat," said Father, pointing at Clyde who sat on the far side of the table, trying to sit up straighter.

Clyde's mother pushed past her husband again and placed the turkey on the table. "I don't care. I want you to carve this damn thing and let's get this meal over with. I've got things to do, too."

Clyde remembered the greasy, buttery aroma spilling out from the roasted turkey. If Father didn't do the carving, Clyde planned to do it himself. He was strong enough.

Father stood in front of the table clenching and unclenching his fists. "Look at this food. How much did this cost me? You forget you're on an allowance? Besides, this kid of ours doesn't need this. Yeah, look at how pitiful he is being catered to like he's a somebody. No one did that for me at his age."

"You're right. Clyde doesn't need this. He doesn't need any of this. I need this for my reputation in this lousy town we're forced to live in because of your crummy job," screamed Mother.

"You stupid woman. I'm a success at my job."

"Don't call me stupid. You can call Clyde that, but don't you dare call me stupid."

"Help me control this lunatic family." Father raised his fists into the air above him as if calling to the heavens for help. As Mother went to the counter to bring more food, Father brought his fists crashing down on top of the dining room table.

The impact sent plates and bowls leaping into the air. Food spilled across the white tablecloth and fell onto the polished linoleum floor. Still fueled by anger, Father swept his arms across the table sending the remaining rich smells and enticing odors plummeting to the floor. Scanning his destructive creation, he glared at Clyde as if daring his son to eat the food on the floor.

Afraid of what his father would do next, Clyde dashed out of the room. On his way out, he slipped on the spilled food and slammed his left knee onto the linoleum floor. In the following weeks and hobbling on a swollen leg, his parents refused to take him to the doctor. With difficulty walking, Clyde sat in the house and began his weight gain.

The commuter train pulled into another station. He held onto the door handle, keeping it opened for people to pass through and get off. Except, Clyde didn't do it for them. He needed to hold on to something for balance.

Pushing his back against the wall, his weight bulged in all directions as people leaned away from his obesity. Finally, the movement of people stopped as the train started moving again.

Scanning the train car, he noted that other commuters were quicker and less sympathetic to his size jumped into seats left by departing passengers. Furious, Clyde knew he would have to wait for the next train stop to get a seat. Can't they see me standing here and not feeling well?

Clyde was tempted to use his size and shove one of the disrespectful people out of their seat. He wanted to yell at someone to let him sit down. If he did any of this, he wouldn't care about being arrested, just being banned from riding the train. He gave a menacing stare across the crowd, but no one paid him any attention. How can people ignore my size?

Probably from clenching the door handle too hard and too long, Clyde flexed his arm trying to get the numbness out. He scowled at the crowd of unsympathetic commuters with hatred. He could not take looking at them any longer.

Frustrated, he shoved his largeness into the vestibule connecting the two train cars. It was hot and noisy there. He continued into the next train car, clenching and unclenching his hand, trying to get the blood flowing again. There had to be an empty seat somewhere, he reasoned.

The frustration ebbed and flowed in Clyde like a roller coaster ride. No one paid him any attention as he passed by. The train car had no available seats, either. Father would not have found himself in this situation, Clyde thought. Father would have controlled his weight, controlled every situation, controlled his life. Yeah, thought Clyde, my father gave me a reason to rebel and not control my eating or my life.

Clyde pushed into the next vestibule and stopped. His sweat felt like flies crawling on his skin. Yet, this was not why he stopped. Amid the clanking and grinding noise where two train cars coupled below his feet, he realized something about his father.

He talked like his father was there in one of the seats. "You were afraid to be loved by anyone, including me. You pretended to love yourself so no one would love you. However, you didn't even love yourself." A few commuters glanced in his direction. Clyde ignored them.

This realization made him temporarily forget his suffering. For a moment, he could think clearly about his father, the man's motivation toward everyone, and how Clyde could deal with it all. With his bulk swaying to the train's movement, Clyde dove into the next car, hoping he would find more truth there.

He didn't care that people paid attention to his excessive flesh flopping past their faces as he charged down the narrow aisle. He only wished he had come to this realization about his father before the man died. I would have told him, "I love you." That would have pissed him off, Clyde thought.

He kept moving, hunting for more truth among the sameness of each car. Entering the next train car, he found empty seats. He did not want them. He wanted to keep searching for more truth.

He pushed further, entering the quiet car. Attempting to sit down, Clyde stumbled and spun like a toy. He finally collapsed onto his back, looking up at a ceiling that would have been the floor if the train was upside down.

His hunger hurt and the throbbing pain in his knee seeped slowly down into his foot and up into his thigh. The pain in his chest struck like needles trying to get out. Sweat stung his eyes until he could not see clearly. Clyde tried to pull his hand up to wipe his face, but it flopped around like a dying fish. Fresh pain became masked by what pain lived there. Pain competed against pain and hurt overtook hurt. In this throbbing intensity, when feelings should not be bearable, Clyde experienced peace.

With his heart pounding aggressively against his chest, trying to escape the suffering and madness sweeping through him, Clyde became happy. His father had a life without love. He died without love. Clyde would not do that. He would live and find love. Hands tried to move him without success. He was too big, and he did not care. There was no fear in him anymore. Instead, euphoria came naturally and wanted.

The pain struggled to come back as Clyde's raspy, shallow breath failed to take in enough air. The chaotic thoughts floating through his mind were like voices calling out for him to survive. Clyde knew what he wanted.

Laughing at how Father would have been appalled to see his fat son splattered across this grimy floor, Clyde called out to him, "Don't worry, Dad. I'll survive and tell people I loved you. I'll lie to them and tell people how you loved me, too." Clyde said this to strangers standing over him. "When I die and meet you across the threshold, you'll know it was me telling people about our love." Clyde figured this was the best way to aggravate his dead father.

A man told Clyde to keep talking because it was keeping him alive. Clyde thought the man was annoying and told him, "I didn't get fat to kill myself. I just didn't like my parents." Clyde swung his arm out and grabbed a woman's hand. "I had love and my parents didn't. They resented me for having something they didn't have."

"Go ahead and love yourself," she replied in a calming tone. She had a pleasant perfume odor mixed with her sweat.

Clyde struggled to get up when the sirens of an ambulance approached. People will be upset I made the train late, he thought with guilt. Then he remembered the train was already late. At some point, he sensed a lot of movement around him. Time seemed to disappear as firm hands lifted his body onto a stretcher. A lot of hands.

He regained consciousness when the surrounding air shifted from a mechanical cool wind to heat and humidity. There was no memory of getting outside. Only the movement of his body and the closeness of people breathing heavily from lifting him. Clyde wondered what train stop he was at.

Before reaching the waiting ambulance, he heard the train horn toot twice as it pulled away. At that moment, may be distracted by the toot, the rescue workers cried out in alarm. They struggled to hold on to the stretcher and keep it upright. But it had lodged on a piece of hot tar.

Clyde's heavy body rolled onto the asphalt like lard rolling around in a frying pan. The hot tar jolted him with pain, meaning he was still alive. He sat up and laughed.

"I love you, rescuers," Clyde yelled to the people trying to get him off the hot pavement.

More people are coming to help, they said.

"More people for me to love," he told them.

Paula and Betty

In preparation to board the train, commuters clumped in small groups along the station platform where the doors would likely open. It was a late spring afternoon with blue skies, warm temperatures, and without the dreaded humidity. The air was too comfortable to be crowding into a metal box.

When the train arrived and before stepping up the metal stairs, Paula spied a silver-haired woman in the next group about to step into the train, too. She turned toward Paula with an open smile that made her eyes smile, too. This woman nodded to Paula before disappearing inside. Paula took the cue and went through her train car and into the next one where she found the woman saving her an aisle-side seat.

"I'm glad you found me. I'm Betty. I don't see you on the train very often."

"I'm Paula. I only ride the train two or three times a week. The other days I work from home. I'm an administrator for one of the think tanks in town."

"I work for a think tank, too, as an international analyst. I think the problem with this city is there are too many people thinking."

Paula smiled. "I agree. I haven't seen you on the train before."

"I haven't been riding the train long," said Betty. "My divorce was finalized a few years ago and I decided recently that I had enough of the city. It's a place to make good money, but expensive to live there. Now, I just tolerate the commute. I wanted to ask you about your artist group. I was not meaning to eavesdrop, but I overheard you talking about it to other women."

"I figured that. People hear things on a crowded train. Besides, my group is not a secret."

Passengers moved around looking for seats or a good place to stand. Some already decided that sitting on the stairs leading to the upper section was a quiet place to ride. They brought pads to sit on. Paula envied them. They had become a single universe among a larger universe of people.

"How did your group get started? I'm always interested in the beginning of things," Betty said, as an explanation.

Paula waited as people pushed past. She recognized people who were not commuters. There were students, tourists, and some who just enjoyed riding the train. Finally, the train lurched forward and people sat or stood somewhere as if the music stopped in a game of musical chairs.

"My group started after my husband Sam and the other men in the neighborhood got into sports. It gave me a chance to talk with other neighborhood women." They were both twisted slightly toward each other making the conversation more between them and not for others who could listen if they wanted.

"So, along came the artist group," Betty said.

"We meet in my house after the men go off for their sporting event. I rearrange the living and dining rooms to give us plenty of room," said Paula.

"I'm assuming you don't get the sports thing and your husband probably doesn't understand your artist group."

Paula smiled. "It's good we have different interests. I can't complain about his sports and he can't complain about my art."

An Amtrak flashed past their window, racing in the opposite direction. The sudden appearance of a fast-moving train startled Paula. It took only a few moments to disappear along the train tracks.

Paula continued. "Sam is my second husband. My first husband ran off with a woman years ago and I haven't heard from him since. I didn't bother with getting child support. I wanted to be done with him. Sam's a great stepdad to my son Jerry, who wants to drive trains when he grows up," said Paula. She felt relaxed with Betty. It was easy talking to her. They talked about the people at their jobs until the next station stop. People pushed past Paula.

When the train moved again, Betty said, "When I look at all these passengers, I'm reminded of a photo I saw a few years ago. It was of a gray suited diver floating alone in blue-green water among colorful fish. He looked out of place. On this commute, I sometimes think of myself as that diver. One who doesn't belong among all that beauty."

Paula thought that was an odd thing to admit after just meeting. Finally, she said, "Maybe that's why I started my artist group. For people who don't belong."

"That's what I thought."

"Do you want to come? You only need to ask."

"Maybe one day. Right now I'm taking college classes in the evening and I don't think I'll have the time. Thanks for asking."

"Why did you want to know about my group?" Paula was getting suspicious.

"I saw some paintings, watercolors, pottery, and macrame in a store near my home. The owner told me where it came from. I liked how everything appeared unique. Your group produces art that I appreciate, and I'm always curious how people come up with their creations. When I meet artists, they usually say the inspiration just came to them."

Paula thought about Angie and how she also loved the art her group produced. "It could be the energy of us getting together that takes over. I'd tell you more, but people may be listening."

Betty turned to the people behind them and asked, "Is anyone back there listening to us?" No one answered. She leaned across Paula and asked the people on the other side and again to the people in front of them.

A balding man with a few wisps of hanging dark hair representing his comb-over poked his head through the seat gap. He had a bushy mustache that angled downward like Tom Selleck's. "I'm trying to sleep," he said.

With an exasperated sigh, Betty dug around in the large satchel at her feet and pulled out two folded seat pads. Paula wondered what else the bag held. And why did Betty carry two seat pads in her bag?

"Let's go to the vestibule where the train cars are hooked together," said Betty.

She stood up and Paula got out of her way since Betty appeared pretty determined.

Where the train cars connected was noisy, dirty, and darker with less ventilation. Fortunately, the better weather outside made the temperature inside tolerable. Both sides of the vestibule had metal stairs going down toward exit doors, depending on what side the station was on. They sat on one set of metal stairs.

"No one can hear us here," said Betty.

"I can hardly hear us."

The vestibule floor moved so much that Paula wondered how the train stayed on the tracks. Apparently, the passenger cars had more support than she realized. Although, the movement in the vestibule was a rocking motion that felt safe.

"Did you plan for us to come out here?" Paula wondered why she followed Betty. Their inside seats were a lot more comfortable.

"No, certainly not. I don't plan or organize. I do it at work and home to keep things simple for me. This pad I keep to sit on because sometimes I come in the vestibule to be by myself. It's noisy and smelly in here, but it's the same as having my private universe. I always take an extra pad as a backup in case someone joins me."

Paula wondered about having a friendship with Betty. None of her friends were like her.

"So, what about this energy in your group?" Betty leaned against a metal pole.

"I want people to be uninhibited. I want them to have confidence in what they create. While I don't encourage it, some women feel their creative energy more by stripping off their bras. But they keep their panties on." Paula smiled, thinking how some of them danced better without clothes.

"Sounds like a fun group. Do you think ghosts help influence anyone's creativity? I'm asking because I read how some writers think they connect with the spiritual world when they create. It's the only explanation they can come up with besides saying the inspiration just came to them."

"I'm not sure about the ghosts. It could also be the chardonnay or the shedding of emotions. I try to bring out as much freedom in everyone that I can."

Paula watched a conductor enter the vestibule, but he said nothing to them. He went to the other set of metal stairs, maybe to give them privacy. It might violate train rules to be in the vestibule, yet he didn't seem to care. It could be common for passengers to sit in the noisy and smelly area where train cars connected, Paula thought. Or maybe he recognized Betty.

"We have about ten minutes to the next stop. Do you believe in ghosts?" Betty looked content sitting on the thin pad amid the rattling.

"Why are you asking me about ghosts?" Paula asked cautiously.

"A week ago on the train, I got the feeling that there were ghosts hanging around you. I know this sounds made up, but sometimes I can be sensitive to these things."

Paula hesitated before explaining, "I live in a blue-collar neighborhood with a creek on two sides, tracks on another side, and the main road on the other. Along with my other neighbors, I have a small garden to pick in. Most are too involved in living to believe in ghosts, although I do. Do you see these ghosts?" Paula wondered if Betty was being serious.

"No, actually I rarely see anything. I sense them, though. Like if I'm walking down a sidewalk and pass an old building, I know someone is still there waiting for something. But I never felt ghosts associated with a person like you. Maybe the energy of your group comes from you attracting ghosts?"

"It could be just your imagination. That's what people always tell me when I see or feel these things," Paula said.

Betty said, "When I was three or four, I started telling my

parents about the people I saw in our house. It was an old place and well kept over the years. They decided I was making up friends since no one my age lived on our street. I was young and didn't know any better. When I was in first grade, we had show-and-tell and I told the class about my ghost friends. Their laughter was enough to keep me from telling anyone else ever again."

"You're talking about them now, so I guess you got over it?"

"In college, people thought I was expressing myself and encouraged it. Later, my first husband tried to use it in our divorce to say I was crazy. So, I'm careful with what I say to who and when. With you, I feel comfortable talking about it."

"Let me tell you about my husband Sam. He's a pretty down-to-earth guy, does woodworking, and is a part-time nurse at the hospital. I like it that he helps me with Jerry. He knows that I sometimes attract ghosts. It doesn't bother me that he doesn't believe, although I think he does but won't admit it. I don't know about my son, and if he has what I have or believes in ghosts. I don't push anyone," said Paula.

"I enjoy telling you about my ghost thing. At least you understand," said Betty.

"There's another part. I believe there are ghosts or spirits or lost souls or whatever people want to call them following the train tracks. I don't know why, maybe the steel attracts them. As I live next to the tracks, I think the ghosts stop by for a visit when my artist group meets." Paula wondered what passengers would think if they heard this conversation.

"Hold on, ladies," said the conductor.

The rattling grew louder before the train lurched to one side, then the other, changing tracks. They both held on to what metal structure they could find. Betty appeared to be better at hanging on. When the rocking subsided, the train slowed down, coming into the next train station.

"We need to get up and move out of the way," said Paula.

"We're okay. The other set of doors where the conductor is standing will open," said Betty.

The train jolted to a stop. Paula waited with Betty as people went by, not paying them any attention. The passengers' focus was getting out of the metal box as fast as possible. Only a few people got on, reluctantly.

When the train started again, the conductor went inside one of the train cars, leaving Betty and Paula alone.

"Why are you taking classes?" Paula wanted their talk redirected to more everyday events.

"I enjoy learning and being with people who want to learn, too. That's why I take courses in the evening. Working people are there while the young are out partying. But back to the ghosts, I think we should hold a séance on the train to see what we'd get. It'll be fun."

Paula grinned, thinking that inviting ghosts to ride with them would scare away passengers and make more seats available. "If ghosts are riding the rails, they can be elusive to know even with a séance. But okay."

For the rest of the trip, they planned their séance. Before getting off, they asked a conductor what was the best train to try it on. He gave them a recommendation. It was a train he was not a conductor on.

That Friday evening and on the last train out of the city, Betty and Paula sat in the rear car waiting until one stop was left. Two men sat near the front facing each other across the aisle with a makeshift table of backpacks on their laps. They were playing cards. Another guy sat in the middle of the train car near the emergency exit window. As soon as the train pulled out of the next-to-last station, Betty stood up near the back and announced they were doing a séance.

The two men left the train car except the guy by the emergency exit window.

"I'm Phil. I'm not sure about this, but it's been a boring ride all week and I've been looking for an adventure."

Paula thought Phil was trying to build up courage to stay away from the emergency exit window. Being part of a séance certainly took courage.

"Good, we need at least three people," said Betty. "We can't have real candles, but I have battery operated ones. Our mood will be the rocking of this train car. We have ten minutes to the next stop. You want to hold hands with us?" Betty wiggled her fingers toward Phil.

He moved over to them and all three stood holding hands next to the last door with a window out the back of the train showing where the train had been. It was too dark to see outside unless they passed some train signal. Betty closed her eyes and started with the yoga chant, "Om."

Paula and Phil looked at each, saying nothing. Paula sensed Phil wished he was back by his emergency exit window.

Several minutes went by and Betty's voice sounded hoarse with all those oms. Paula was about to take over when she heard something. With Betty keeping her eyes closed, Paula and Phil looked at the opposite end of the train car where they spied a balding man with strands of dark hair flat across his head. A bushy mustache framed his mouth, angled downward the same as Tom Selleck's.

"I got tired of riding in the quiet car and wanted to see what was at the other end of this train," said the man.

"You want to join us?" asked Paula.

"No, you're holding hands like in a séance. I just want to

say that Claudia was not all bad. She was confused about love. Sheila was bad and did not care or understand about relationships, but she'll learn. Wanda couldn't help loving Harry. They need each other more than anyone can know."

"How do you know about my *former* commuters?" Phil stared at the man.

"Who are those people?" Paula asked, looking at Phil. "Do you know this guy?"

"No, I don't know him. Do you know him? Is this all a joke? Why would anyone go to this much trouble to play a joke on me?" Phil jerked his hands away.

Betty kept her eyes closed, still doing that "om" thing. The moonless night made the train windows even darker, leaving Paula to consider they could be the only people left in the universe. Nothing could be seen except the neon lights creating a beam down the narrow aisle to the other end where the man used to stand. He had left the train car without Paula or Phil seeing him leave. Betty finally stopped her oms and opened her eyes.

"I think our stop is coming up," said Betty, yawning. "Sorry, I got sleepy with the train rocking and everything quiet. I kept thinking about the name 'Luis.' How was it with you two?"

Phil glanced at the two women as if expecting them to explain. Paula stared back, expecting an explanation from Phil. With all the staring, Phil stumbled toward his seat where he grabbed his backpack and ran up to queue alone.

"That mustache guy from a few days ago came into the train car and told Phil about some people he knew," Paula explained to Betty.

"Did Phil know him?"

"No, he thought we were playing a joke on him," said

Paula.

Betty yawned again. "I see he's ignoring us. Maybe we can try this again some other time with another person."

"I think once is enough for me. That mustache guy gave me the creeps. He didn't seem real."

Betty gathered up her battery operated candles and said, "Maybe I will come to your artist group tonight, if you don't mind. I've been doing oil painting and I could use some critical eyes at what I create."

"Sure," said Paula. "But we'll keep the ghost thing to ourselves for the first few times, at least."

"Sure," said Betty with a smile.

Voyages Home: A Week on the Commuter Train

Monday Meeting

In the evening, Tony stood on the train station platform amid a gathering flock of commuters who somehow managed to *not* block a chilly wind from blowing his way. A few minutes before, an Amtrak sped by leaving a grand torrent of wind that made him and everyone else colder. The Amtrak was ten minutes late, meaning his commuter train would be twenty minutes late. Train companies tracked time like a *Twilight Zone* or *Outer Limits* episode.

Tony glanced to his right at a stylishly figured, tall woman who nudged next to him, apparently trying to use Tony to block the wind. Her thick, silvery hair landed behind her shoulders in a gentle ponytail. Like himself, she was one big blanket of coat and scarf. Like everyone else, she watched the empty steel rails before them remain empty.

The 4:55 train rumbled to a stop at 5:15, right on time for a late train. Tony could not believe his luck at having the set of doors open in front of him. He would have his first choice of seats. Like water swirling down a narrow spout, other commuters followed him up the metal stairs and into the warm train car. Warm more from the mass of bodies than the sparse artificial heat. He noticed the silver-haired woman behind him.

Tony's luck held and he spied the last empty set of dual seats. All the other seats were aisle side and this was the only one offering a coveted window seat. Something to lean against when he went to sleep. However, Tony did a rare commuter thing and let the silver-haired woman in first. She accepted his offer with a thank-you smile that made her eyes smile, too.

Tony had no clue why he did this. If he fell asleep in an aisle side seat, he risked falling on the floor. Yet, he had little hope of sleep with people bumping into him as they passed by with their bags and backpacks and overweight accumulation of clothing. At least I won't sleep past my stop, he thought. Meanwhile, the woman settled into her window seat as if floating down on top of feather pillows.

Settling in his aisle side seat, Tony twisted his wedding ring around on his finger. Finally, he plucked it off and put it in his pants pocket. Each time he held the ring, he thought about the good times with his wife before her death years ago. He wondered when it would be a good time to take it off for good.

His daughter Carolyn, who lived at home with him, did not want him wearing the wedding ring. She was all about moving on and he worried one day she would move on and take his granddaughter Alice to live somewhere else. As the train pulled out of the station, Tony recalled last night's supper with Carolyn, Alice, and the inquisitive dog Mary.

"Stop worrying about how you'll always be a widower. I

lost a mother and I'm finding a way out of my grief through Paula's art class," Carolyn told her dad. They sat at the kitchen table across from plates of spaghetti. "You need to find a hobby where you can meet people instead of hiding in the garage doing your carvings."

"What is Paula teaching you exactly?" Tony ignored Carolyn's comment about his lack of sociability.

"She's letting us discover our own creativity. Paula gives us a place where we can talk, laugh, and cry. But not in that order."

"Okay, then where does Joey fit in?"

"He's Paula's cousin and shows up sometimes and gives us snacks he's made. He's getting a doctorate in some engineering area and moved here to work at the new manufacturing plant outside of town. He's a little goofy, but tolerable. And a great pastry cook."

Tony wondered when Joey would show up at supper. He wondered when he would be eating supper alone.

At the next station stop, Tony glanced at the woman next to him. She continued to be absorbed in a thick book lying across her lap. As the train headed to another station, Tony got out his e-reader to read a library book he was glad he hadn't purchased.

Approaching the station, Tony asked the woman, "Do you get off at this stop?" She looked like she was falling asleep and he did not want her sleeping past her stop like he did sometimes.

"No, not here." She was kind in her reply as she turned a page with a careful motion.

She's studying a textbook, Tony concluded. Another stop later and Tony thought for sure she had fallen asleep reading her book. He asked her, "Do you get off here?"

"No, not here," she said, not looking up from her hardcover.

Tony wondered why she would lug such a heavy book on the commute. Didn't she have an e-reader?

Fifteen minutes later at the next stop, she asked mischievously, "Do you get off here?" She did not look up from her book.

"No, not here," he replied, smiling.

"Where do you get off?"

"Next to the last stop, deep in suburbia. And you?" Tony caught a wisp of her sweet perfume.

"At the end of the line. I ride from beginning to end."

"But you got on at my stop."

She closed her book and paid him better attention. "I was in the area for a meeting and didn't want to go back to my office."

She had brown eyes, high cheekbones, and a small, straight nose. She pulled her lips apart in an open smile that helped frame her rich, dark olive skin.

"What do you do? Work, I mean." Tony wanted to continue their talk.

"I work for one of the think tanks in the city. Mostly in international affairs. My specialty is eastern Europe. What about you?"

"I'm a human resource analyst for the government. Mostly I work in human relationships," said Tony.

"That could be a challenge in this city."

Tony thought about all the secrets he found out and told no one about. Many times he felt like a priest doing confession. "A lot of my job is keeping people who are not married to each other from having sex with each other in their offices. I'm thinking of switching to training and development. It's more straightforward and people aren't crying and yelling. You have a husband or children?"

"I have an ex-husband and no children. Our breakup lasted our whole marriage. We finalized it a few years ago, so I don't mind anymore. What about you?"

"My wife died a few years ago, so I don't understand divorce." Tony frightened himself by admitting his wife's death to a stranger. This woman was too easy to talk to.

"Even at my age, I don't understand death as well as I should. I'm sorry for your loss."

"It was years ago. My daughter and granddaughter live with me along with my dog. Everything has mostly worked out."

"Names?"

"My daughter is Carolyn, my granddaughter is Alice, and my dog is Mary."

"I'm Betty."

"I'm Tony."

"I appreciate you not asking why I don't have any children," said Betty. "I don't think every woman needs to have a child. Instead, I have a niece from my older brother and a nephew from my younger sister. I'm the oldest and everything works out better that way."

"I appreciate you not asking about Alice's father. He's gone now. Carolyn and he never married, which was a good thing since he preferred his alcohol and drugs to her." Tony shifted slightly in his seat to face Betty better. Her complexion seemed to glow from the inside. He could tell she had a slight Asian look to her eyes and cheeks that gave her a soft, peaceful look.

"Have you tried other ways to commute other than by train?" Betty asked.

Tony grinned. "I've done all the ways there are. I drove alone, took a bus, joined a van pool, and did carpooling. I also tried slugging, which is actually a form of hitchhiking. All these ways put me on the roads and I think the rails are the best way to commute."

"I recently moved from the city and have only ridden the train. When it doesn't run, I work from home. Commuting is stressful enough and I'm not into alternative means of travel."

They settled into a conversation about train adventures, of which Tony had plenty to tell. After several more stops, the train slammed to a stop hundreds of feet from Tony's station. The only movement was the wind in the trees outside their window, as if waving them hello. Ten minutes later, Carolyn called.

"My daughter said they're having signal problems," Tony said to Betty.

"I think they may have already announced that."

"I saw a couple of people get off the train and walk the tracks to the station. It's right over there. I think I'll do that, too. You want to come? I can give you a ride to your station."

"I'll take my chances and stay. They can't leave this train sitting here forever."

Tony wished he could stay and continue talking to Betty, but he remembered the frustration in Carolyn's voice after comforting a child who was teething. He followed other commuters off the train. The conductors said nothing as they were equally frustrated with the train dispatcher who was located over a thousand miles away at a computer terminal.

For ten minutes, Tony followed a line of aggravated commuters down an access road to the station. As he climbed onto the station platform to head for the parking lot, he heard a horn toot twice and looked behind him. The train was pulling into the station. From her window, Betty waved. Tony waved back.

Tuesday Learning

The next evening, Tony stood in the same spot on the station platform, waiting for the same train he waited for every evening. Betty was not with him, having no meeting in the area.

He pulled off his wedding ring and held it in his hand for a few seconds before slipping it into his pocket. I should have a ceremony at home to remove it permanently, he considered. I'd have Mary attend. As a dog, she somehow understands these things. Or I think she does. Tony thought about it, but he wouldn't invite Carolyn. He told her he was not wearing the ring anymore and having a ceremony to remove it might disappoint her.

On the train, Betty saved a place for Tony by placing her thick book and heavy coat in the aisle seat. She wore a pale red dress with a multi-colored sash thrown around her neck and left shoulder. Her hair was still in a ponytail. She picked up her book and draped her coat across her lap when he appeared.

"People probably assumed my book and coat belonged to someone in the bathroom," Betty said when Tony asked.

"Why would they think that?"

"Because I told them when they asked."

Tony smiled. "Thanks for saving me the seat. What's your book about?"

"I'm taking a course at the community college about cultural anthropology. We're studying archeology first and linguistics in the second part. I'm also taking philosophy and religion on Thursday. I want to know where I came from and if I should bother understanding anything while I'm here."

"I took World History last semester," Tony said. He caught a faint wisp of her perfume, or he hoped it was hers. There were lots of commuter smells on the train from all these people.

"What period of history did you study?" She twisted her body toward him more.

"The French Enlightenment. We discussed Mary Wollstonecraft's *A Vindication of the Rights of Woman*. I really enjoyed discussing her argument for women's rights at the same time men were arguing for their rights against the aristocracy. What about your class?"

"We're studying recent discoveries from the excavations of barrows and kitchen middens in Europe. I enjoy reading about those discoveries. They show layers of everyday life, all from the view of a person's trash heap."

"In my history class, I learned to see human life trying to connect toward a fairer and better future."

Betty asked, "After commuting, where do you think you'll be? I always picture myself standing in sunshine on a warm, uncrowded beach of soft sand."

"I see myself buried in too many starts and not enough finishes on things I've always wanted to do." Tony wanted to tell Betty how he planned a future with his wife Mary, taking naps together wherever she wanted. "But I have hope that I'll be wrong and I find my destiny."

"Maybe your granddaughter is your destiny," Betty said.

Tony had a lot to say about Alice and Betty had a lot of questions. At the end, he said, "I have too many regrets for not spending more time with Carolyn when she was growing up. I hope to fix that with Alice. I also have my dog Mary, who I think is smarter than me."

Tony did not tell Betty that his wife's name was Mary, too. He didn't want to explain that it had nothing to do with Mary. The dog, not his wife.

"Your stop is coming up. I'll see you tomorrow," said Betty.

"I'll look for you."

Outside, the cold air blew in Tony's face. He stood on the concrete platform, watching departing passengers head for their vehicles. After the train pulled away in a fit of diesel fumes, he found himself alone listening to the sound of those vehicles running out of the parking lot. He soon followed them in his car, eager to get home to his family.

Wednesday The Arts

A strong, chilly wind blew across the train station platform, making Tony wish he had won the lottery. Everyone tried to use someone else to block the wind and Tony was losing the competition. He stood there trying to forget another day of work memories.

He thought about how he was always on the move. Always traveling to work or home and feeling like he never reached either place before he had to leave again. Almost on time, a thunder of noise and a rush of more cold air arrived. The shiny steel rails before him filled with the long commuter train that was not too too late. Tony wondered why it was always late on days when the weather was worse.

Pushing himself down the narrow aisle of the train car, he spied Betty keeping a seat for him again. She sat on the aisle side, preventing people from sitting in the window seat. Her courageousness over other commuters who demanded to sit by the window impressed him. Betty scooted to the window seat to make it easier for Tony to sit in her warm spot.

"I thought I'd try a different technique this evening. The other way worked better," Betty said as Tony sat down.

"Window seats are too desirable for commuters. There's usually plenty of unwanted aisle seats," said Tony.

"I thought more people would like the aisle side. They can escape the train more easily," Betty said.

"That's true. But there's more who want a window to look out of since all they see during the day is the inside of a building."

The train jumped to a start toward the next station. Some people in the aisle still looking for a seat had a moment of unbalance. They saved themselves from falling by bumping into people in the aisle seats, who looked disgruntled at the stumbler. Tony tried not to laugh at the stumblers and sitters.

"At least I have a window. It looks out at an oak tree. It's old enough to have seen the start of the twentieth century," said Betty.

"I admire trees of all kinds. They have patiently lived through all kinds of history. I think of Carolyn, Alice, and Mary as my trees. Always there to keep my life consistent and contently complicated in a controlled chaos."

"I think everyone needs some orderly chaos in their lives to keep from thinking they have control. I surround myself with chaotic things I don't understand, so I stay somewhat confused and challenged. If I figure things out, it's as if I discovered a new world and accomplished something in it. I achieve hypersanity."

"I need to try that." Tony watched Betty's brown eyes and he glimpsed a look of confidence in her. He wondered if hypersanity was the same as mindfulness.

They continued talking about books, movies, plays, and how they enjoyed talking about the arts rather than commuting or their jobs.

"I carve wood from trees that died naturally and before decay sets in. This may sound odd, but I look for some final, remaining memory in their heartwood. I believe that when living trees are cut down, the trauma makes them lose their memories and the wood is no good for carving."

"What do you carve?" Betty raised an eyebrow, interested in Tony's beliefs.

"Whatever the tree wants," he said. "I know this sounds strange, but there always seems to be a memory left in the wood I try to find. Sometimes I end up adding more and more detail."

"I'd like to see your carvings sometime. They seem motivating."

"People think the carvings come out too abstract and that they have no recognizable shape. It could be a miscommunication between me and the wood. I could also be imagining the whole thing. Yeah, that would be okay if you want to see them sometime." Tony considered Betty coming to supper one evening.

Tony's stop came before he could finish explaining that the wood he carved made him feel like he could stop commuting one day.

Thursday A Ring

Waiting for the evening train, Tony pictured the commuters around him as a line of headaches waiting for the end of the work week that seemed to take all week to come. They hid their misery beneath coats and scarves, continuing to be strangers while sharing the same desire to end their commute one day.

Tony did not ride Betty's morning train with her as it left his station a little after five in the morning. His schedule included taking care of Mary and helping Carolyn with Alice. He matched their schedule instead of Betty's.

That evening as diesel fumes thundered in front of him, Tony's luck held and the metal doors slid open in front of him. When he turned into the train car, he spotted Betty's friendly smile and large brown eyes. She saved the aisle seat with a coat, scarf, and her hand to make sure no one touched them.

"What's your Philosophy and Religion class like?" Tony asked as he sat down. He needed time to slip off his wedding ring. The evening before, he'd forgotten to take it off and Carolyn had noticed. Tony didn't want another argument about moving on when he got home.

"It has to do with finding faith and belief. The class is also about trying to get from one place to another safely and happily. Much like riding this train."

For some reason, the ring would not budge. He stopped struggling since it was apparent what he was doing. He kept his right hand over his finger, pretending nothing was amiss by holding hands with himself.

Betty continued, "From my class, I've concluded that people pray to God by following some philosophical life or performing mundane rituals. What they should do is learn how to pray to God first without ceremony. Maybe then we wouldn't need so many religions fighting religious wars. I've also learned to believe more in meditation, reincarnation, souls, and God, but not in that order. What do you believe in?"

"God and souls in that order. I accept reincarnation and meditation along with alien contact. I don't like to say 'abduction' although that may happen through misunderstanding," Tony said.

"I like to call them extraterrestrials and wish we discussed them in class. I'd like to meet an ET one day."

"Maybe if we weren't riding the train all the time, we'd have a better chance of meeting them," Tony said.

"Maybe they're driving the train," Betty smiled.

Tony talked about all the strange people who could be driving the train and Betty matched him. Their giggling brought annoyed looks from other passengers, so they tried to make a poem about riding the train. Betty saw the train poetically as hugging the edge of the river, slipping across worn bridges, and running over tendrils of small streams. Tony provided imagery with the witness of small birds darting out of the bushes and trees, startled by the noisy train. They talked about these scenes as if not doing so would stop them from existing.

"Yesterday, I forgot to ask if you do anything in the arts," said Tony.

"Starting at the beginning, I got into oil paintings when I was a teenager. But I never told my friends. I was afraid people would laugh at what I made. My parents called my paintings a hobby, but they weren't to me."

"You still have them?"

"No. One day at college, my parents called and said they'd thrown away my paintings. They had mold on them. For a long time I grieved for losing that part of my childhood. But I accepted their loss like I accepted my parents' death and my divorce. Things have a way of changing for the better."

"Does that mean you're still painting?" Tony pictured

Betty in a smock stained with bright oil colors.

"I took it up again after my divorce. It was my therapy. Recently I joined a small group of women artists from the train who are helping me gain confidence. Maybe one day someone will pick up one of my paintings and smile at what they see."

Tony was not sure what to say. Carolyn had said a similar thing about her writing. Obviously they both belonged to the same artist group and must know each other, at least artistically. He hoped Carolyn and Betty had good opinions about each other's work. He was about to tell Betty that Carolyn went to the artist group, too, when the train stopped at an Amtrak station dually used by commuters.

On the platform, a boy and girl held hands as they looked up at the mass of metal and noise dominating their senses. Their parents stood behind them, waving at someone getting off the train. The two children waved to Betty and Tony, who waved back. For unknown reasons, Tony chose that moment to pull off his wedding ring.

It popped off and went sailing into the back of the seat in front of him, ricocheted somewhere off Betty's clothes, and clinked across the hard floor. In horror, Tony heard it continue to clinker like a siren under the seats. He didn't know where it went.

"What did you drop?" Betty's voice sounded hopeful, which Tony needed.

"My wedding ring. It came off." He wished he had not said *wedding*.

"Oh, dear! We've got to find it. It must mean so much to you." Betty stood up and announced, "Everyone, my friend has lost his wedding ring. It's rolled on the floor somewhere. Could everyone please look around for the ring?"

Everyone on the train shifted their focus to the floor. It

was remarkable how Betty could command such authority, Tony thought. He wanted to crawl on the floor, too. Mostly to hide from embarrassment thinking how it looked for him to lose his wedding ring beside someone who was not his wife.

Before the train pulled out of the station, a twenty-something man approached their seat. He had gold and silver rings hanging from his lip, nose, and top and bottom ear lobes. He didn't speak, but held out his palm with Tony's ring, like exposing a trophy.

Tony expected the people on the train car to applaud, but they just resettled back in their seats to continue with their commuting experience as if this thing happened all the time. Betty and he over thanked the ring man, who slipped back to his seat without saying anything. Tony was grateful the ring was not one of the stranger's ornaments.

"That was easy, wasn't it?" Betty slipped the ring onto his finger. Tony wondered if this meant he was married again.

"I want to explain the ring," said Tony as the train started off to the next station.

"You don't need to. It's easier to take a ring off after a divorce."

Two stops later, Tony got off and thanked a smiling Betty and the ring man. On the platform, he waved to Betty as the train left. The ring man waved, too. Distance separated them quickly.

Friday Coming Together

It wasn't as cold Friday evening as Tony stood among a sparser crowd waiting for the train. He was glad more commuters stayed home on Friday claiming telework or having already worked their forty hours that week. He concluded they were just too tired to go on for another day. Adding two to three hours a day to commute created a significant sleep deficit for most people. Tony was grateful for Fridays when he could enjoy being cold and miserable without many people around.

As the train approached, Tony felt good. Not because it was Friday, although that was a very good reason to feel better, but because he had no ring to lose this time. It sat exactly centered on top of his bedroom dresser. When he told Carolyn about how he'd lost the ring, Alice giggled and it looked like Mary smiled. Carolyn just gave him *the look*.

With fewer people riding, Betty easily saved a seat for him. He wondered if it was because other commuters now knew they were riding together. The inside warmth of the train made him sleepy, yet he stayed awake listening to the calm of Betty's voice as she talked about her philosophy and religion class. Tony relaxed with Betty as if he had always known her.

"This train takes us from home and brings us back to think about where we've been," she said. "Philosophy makes me think like this. I don't know what religion makes me think other than what ritual to follow."

"With this long commute, I'm left with the weekend to catch up on stuff. Time is going fast. I feel like I'm being sucked in a time warp."

"But commuting can be enjoyable," said Betty.

"Yeah, you're right. Riding the evening train does give me time to myself and lets me unwind from work. In the morning, it gives me some good sleep time." Tony never had to worry about oversleeping past his stop in the morning because several people set their watch alarms. Tony loosened his tie and undid his top shirt button.

"I think about the people around me. Who they are and how they spend their lives when not riding the train. I know that some have written novels on this trip."

Tony smiled. "I'm glad to get home to a cup of hot tea and a good book. That is, after I help Carolyn with Alice and take Mary for a walk."

A low ridge of vinyl between their train seats provided weak separation. Tony explained his hunt for the emerald ring ghost.

Betty said, "In winter, the only thing I try to look for is the sun. I leave in the dark and come home in the dark. If I didn't go out for lunch and had no window in my cubicle, then daylight might never have happened."

Tony turned in his seat to face Betty better. "I never thought about the ghost looking for me. In any case, we aren't looking for each other anymore."

He noticed they were over halfway home and Tony wanted their conversation to continue. He asked Betty, "We should do something this weekend. Spend time downtown and eat at one of the cafés. We can meet for coffee at the Sasson Café on the corner of Princess Anne and Frederick streets."

Before Betty could respond, the many ton train made a desperate attempt to stop. The sudden braking effort forced Tony and Betty to lunge forward and brace themselves against the back of the seat they faced. Somewhere in the train car, a woman screamed as the train car shivered. A crushing blend of moving metal screamed back.

The lights flashed off before anyone could see what was happening. As the emergency lighting struggled to come on, the grind of metal on metal echoed up and down the train car before quickly stopping. Tony felt the car turn toward the trees. He did not want to go home that way.

One jolt, one shudder, and the train car ceased to move as

abruptly as if it had fallen off a cliff. The emergency lighting flowed across a chorus of human noise as people scrambled to find a way off.

"Let's wait here," said Tony, clutching Betty's tense hand.

"Don't we need to get off?"

"There's no smoke or fire and we're not turned over. The people getting hurt are the ones panicking to get off."

With the exit doors on both ends jammed shut from the twisted train car, people pushed themselves head first through the doors' half window. They landed on the other side with many ugly sounds of pain.

Some commuters pulled off the rubber strips on the emergency window frames, causing the unmanageable heavy windows to fall inside the train car and onto those wanting to be off first. Those people were left under the massive windows as people scrambled to get out.

"I hope those people are not hurt too much," Betty said, watching the panic subside as people realized the only danger was in their panic.

The train's speaker system crackled to life. "Everyone, please stay where you are. We've had a slight derailment after hitting some debris. There is no danger if you stay on the train. We have rescue coming."

"I guess we'll be here awhile," said Tony as he heard sirens in the distance trying to find a path toward them.

"I have a surprise for us," Betty said. "There's two miniature wine bottles in my bag I bought before getting on the train. I planned to have them with supper tonight, but this looks like a good time. You like red?"

"I like wine," Tony said.

Betty smiled. "And, yes, I'd like to have coffee with you tomorrow."

Angie and Phil

While finishing her morning makeup, Angie noticed that the wrinkle she spied last week crouched in the outer corner of her left eye had become a deeper line. A hesitant glance to the other eye exposed a twin and triggered a memory from a week ago she had been trying to forget ever since.

"You're getting more stubborn the older you get. You need to find some love," Angie's mother said over the smartphone.

Angie was glad her mother would rather talk on the phone than visit. Saying these things face-to-face would make their talks even more unpleasant.

"I'm just trying to be a friend by telling you this," Mother persisted.

"I don't want you as my friend. You're too critical." Angie wasn't sure she wanted her as a mother, either. One seemed to be just as critical as the other.

"You need a relationship. You need to get some friends. Stop being so distrustful of people. People don't like someone who abuses themselves like that."

"I'm not distrustful of everyone. Just people like my ex."

"What happened with that actor guy?"

Angie regretted telling her mother about him. Mostly she

regretted having him perform her one-act play and showing how much of a mess she had written. It motivated her to write a better play and not to see the actor anymore. He reminded her too much of her father. Now, there were two men—her ex and the actor—to avoid on the train.

"Are you still there?" her mother asked.

"I'm not seeing him anymore. He was too much like your husband. You should know how that is. You've been distrustful of people ever since he left us for acting gigs in Asia."

"That's what I mean. You don't want to be like me at my age."

"I'm happy like I am. I have friends," Angie said. They were all from Paula's artistic group, but still friends. She used to have friends years ago, but they had children she couldn't have.

Angie remembered Paula's cousin Joey. Their one lunch date was enough for both of them to know more dates would be worse. They agreed that their relationship was safer as friends. Besides, he and that other woman Carolyn were better suited for each other, Angie accepted.

She pushed these memories away and returned to hiding those deep lines around her eyes. Staring at her face, Angie convinced herself she was happy. Happy with the changes to her play, happy there was no pressure to have a family, and happy she could finish her makeup in time to make the crowded commuter train. She could even be happy with those irritating lines around her eyes.

It was a struggle not to be in a foul mood when getting off the train. The mass of humanity inside the train car at such an early hour made her want to be back in bed and catch up on her lack of sleep. When she reached her office building, she competed with too many people for too few elevators. Angie spied Phil crowding into her elevator on the far side.

He rode the same morning and evening train she did, but she liked to move around on the train to avoid her ex and the actor and only saw him occasionally. When she found herself in Phil's train car, she was always amused watching and overhearing his adventures at romance.

Angie watched Phil get off the elevator on her floor. She had only been working at the company for a month, but knew he had a cubicle somewhere in the massive cubicle farm. She just didn't know where. She preferred a chance meeting one day instead of being accused of stalking.

She went in the opposite direction from him toward her cubicle. Along the way, Angie avoided talking to coworkers about the coming weekend. She had nothing to contribute because she had no weekend plans except to work on her play. And that's all right, she thought, as she sat down in her grayish cubicle and found her monitor was missing.

Stepping into the cubicle created hallway, Angie counted the number of cubicles from the break room. All the cubicles had the same look, but this was definitely her cubicle. She leaned against another cubicle wall, trying to figure out how her monitor could be missing and almost pushed the flimsy partition over.

"Hey, watch it," called out a man's voice.

"I was looking for my monitor."

"Did you look in your cubicle?"

"Funny."

"Ask Robert. His monitor broke and he was looking in the empty cubicles for a replacement yesterday evening," said the stranger.

"Damn it," said Angie, walking away. She found Robert using her monitor. It had her name taped across the top.

"What's wrong with you? You took my monitor," Angie yelled at Robert's pudgy, bald head.

"I got it from an empty cubicle."

"That was my cubicle and it wasn't empty. There was stuff all over it."

"I thought it was just a storage area. I didn't see any pictures or anything personal there."

"I don't care. Give me back my monitor."

Fifteen minutes later, Angie stared at her monitor, unable to concentrate on her work. She scanned her cubicle space, thinking what personal items she could put there. There was nothing she could think of. Anything I put in here might lead coworkers to think I could get personal with them, she thought.

"I see you found your monitor," said Phil, standing at her cubicle entrance.

"How did you know I was looking for it?" Angie wished the cubicles had doors.

"That was my wall you almost pushed over."

Angie glared at Phil for intruding into her space. "Your wall is still standing."

"I didn't know you worked here. I've seen you on the train before and I thought of a nickname for you. You're Angie in the Clouds."

"Don't call me that. I don't want a nickname."

"Don't you want to know why I nicknamed you that?"

"No."

"On the train you always seem like you have your head in the clouds."

"That's a cliché and I don't like them."

"Sometimes clichés are useful. Like when I use them to nickname fellow commuters." Phil smiled and walked away before Angie could tell him how she wished she had pushed his wall over.

Angie spent several hours emailing documents to her coworkers for comments and getting nothing back until her monitor flashed a warning that a priority email had arrived. It wanted her decision on something she did not care about. She stared at the words in the email without giving the flat glass any verdicts.

Irritated with her work that morning and the priority email, she got up and walked to Phil's cubicle. Since her day had been a mess so far, Angie decided not to have lunch alone again. Phil seemed as good as anyone. Except, a nearby cubicle mate said he had already gone to lunch.

Frustrated, Angie went back to her cubicle. She passed Tony sitting in his cubicle and she remembered he was the guy on the train looking for that emerald ring ghost. Angie wondered if she should be looking for ghosts, too. No, she thought, I have enough ghosts from my past following me around on the train already.

At her cubicle, Angie snatched a mirror out of her drawer, searching for those irritating wrinkles and hoping they had disappeared. Instead, she surveyed her long bob haircut and fringy bangs. When she had it done, she thought it made her look strong, resilient, and forthright. She didn't like the word "forthright" anymore. It was time for a change. Angie took her lunch time to find a hairdresser she could trust.

At the end of the workday, she left before Phil and waited on the station platform for the evening train. The new job put her on the train several stops before her ex and the actor got on. There was no need to travel to another station to avoid them.

At this station, heavy winter coats separated everyone. Angie added more separation by keeping back a step or two from the yellow caution strip, unlike those on both sides of her who ventured impatiently to the edge. The space in front helped control a fear she had that a crowd was stalking her. She could contain her anxiety with that small space before her.

She was okay like this until an annoying man, covered in a coat and hood, hustled himself down the yellow strip in front of the crowd. He stopped in front of Angie, exactly in the small space she left between her and the yellow caution strip. Before she could use her favorite list of angry expletives, the roar of the commuter train thundered into view and dominated everything. When the train stopped, the hooded man blocked everyone and allowed Angie to board first. Like an apology, commuter style.

Angie ignored him and hurried up the metal stairs, almost tripping. Inside, she plopped into a window seat. Yet, it gave the hooded man the opportunity to plop down beside her in the aisle seat. With a brush of his hand, he slipped off his hood.

"I knew it had to be you," Angie said to Phil. The hood had made a mess of his brown hair. "Commuters have no patience for foolishness at the end of a long day."

She ran her hand through long and short sections of her hair, trying to arrange everything differently until giving up and placing her hands in her lap. I would have been better shaving my head and starting over, she thought.

"Don't worry. I won't push my luck. I'm an experienced commuter myself."

"I'm not worried about you. I don't want my train late from a riot you might cause," Angie said.

"I wouldn't want that, either. I'd be late getting home,"

said Phil. "Anyway, why were you looking for me at lunch?"

"I was rude to you before and I thought you could show me some good places to eat."

"Why don't we have lunch on Monday?" Phil shifted in his seat, trying to get comfortable.

"I may be busy with a priority email."

"We all get those emails. They're from a former train rider Clyde, who works on another floor of our building. He's been working here ever since his heart attack and you should see him now. He's lost a lot of weight."

"I know him! He's helped me on the train before."

"He won't be helping you on the train anymore. He moved into the city with this guy I nicknamed Standing Slim. You've probably used to see him standing in the rear of the train."

"Yeah, I remember him. He's not the same guy you called Don't Jump Ben, is he?" Angie gave Phil a slight smile.

"Nah, that guy and some woman Claudia were caught having sex in a train bathroom. They got kicked off." Phil looked at Angie curiously. "How did you know about that nickname?"

"You talk to yourself sometimes on the train. I sat behind you when the seat notice came out that the bathrooms were for one person at a time. You guessed it was Ben." Angie scooted in a better position to face Phil. "But what about Clyde and this other guy and what's his real name?"

"Hey, I don't know all the gossip on the train."

Angie smiled a little more. "You're the gossip king. I'm serious. I want to know if Clyde will be okay."

"I'll tell you since I want to tell someone and it's really not a secret. I heard from several passengers that one morning Clyde stood up and announced he was gay. Woke everyone up, but it was time for people to wake up, anyway."

Angie giggled. "That sounds like Clyde. But what's Standing Slim's name? I've seen you two having wine in the back of the train on Friday evenings."

"His name is Luis. He said he was named after some Spanish relative who fought in some civil war. He was married and never felt right about it. A few days after Clyde's announcement, he announced he was gay. He's not married anymore. He and Clyde are now lovers. They moved into a city apartment with a guy named Ernie who also used to ride the train. Coincidentally, he was married to Claudia, the bathroom sex queen. Clyde makes his emails a priority to rush people so he won't be stuck at work any longer than he wants. He wants to spend time with Luis."

"I'm not surprised about Clyde. I'm really happy for him."

"If you see him, don't be surprised if he tells you he loves you. He says that to everyone since his heart attack."

The train stopped at a station where they watched people struggle with their bags and backpacks to get on and off. When the train started moving again, Phil asked Angie, "What about lunch Monday? Not answering Clyde's priority email won't stop him from going home on time. Besides, we shouldn't put lunch off. All this commuting speeds up time and, before you know it, years have passed."

"That makes no sense." However, Angie wondered how many years she'd been riding the train, too. It seemed like the train schedule had been the only stable thing in her life for too many years.

"I've been riding so long I wrote a novel. I may have written more and not realized it."

"Did you publish it?"

"I hope to, soon. I overheard you and Paula on the train.

You joined her artist group. Maybe you can get me an invite and they can critique my novel."

"I don't think so. It's all women and they like to express themselves creatively sometimes." Angie thought Phil's attention felt right. Her frustration earlier with him seemed ridiculous.

"I remember you were writing a play. Is that what you do in the group?"

"Yeah, I'm rewriting my play," she said.

"With that actor guy I saw you with?"

"No. Definitely no. I won't be going back to that theater, either. Too many bad memories."

"Okay, then why don't we share what we've written. We could be each other's beta reader."

"I don't want you criticizing my stuff. I don't think it's ready. But I don't mind criticizing your stuff." Angie did not mind the women providing criticism. They were like a family. She wondered about her offer to Phil. It made her think about opening doors and letting her fears and distrust of relationships fly away.

"Good, we can set something up. Writing helps me cope with all this commuting. By the way, weren't you with some guy from that group named Joey?"

"You jump from subject to subject a lot. Yeah, we dated once. You dated that woman who talked on her cell all the time."

"Yeah, thankfully that's over. She didn't like my phone etiquette." Phil smiled and shook his head as if trying to shake the memory away.

"I'm sure you'll find someone and have kids one day," said Angie.

"No kids for me. That's why my first wife left. I'm sterile."

Phil opened his mouth into a massive yawn, causing Angie to yawn, too.

"But you probably want to adopt," said Angie.

"I don't know. Never thought that much about it. But I'm game if someone else is. If I nod off, I know of an Italian restaurant we could go to this evening," Phil said. "The chef makes a pasta sauce I can eat without regret the next day."

"Maybe we could do that tomorrow night. This is Friday and I have Paula's group to go to tonight," said Angie. It came out before she stopped herself. She kept thinking about how he was like her and couldn't have kids.

"That sounds better. We can meet early and walk around downtown." Phil gave off another yawn, more exaggerated. "We can do lunch on Monday, too. I'll invite Roger."

"Okay, I'll bring my monitor."

Phil slipped into a silence that felt like a scream to Angie. Within a few moments, he had scooted down in his seat and closed his eyes without even a goodnight. He was asleep by the time they left the next station and did it so quickly that Angie got angry.

"I don't like people sleeping next to me on the train," Angie said, leaning close to Phil's face. She liked how he smelled. Maybe having him sleep next to me would be okay, she thought. His steady breathing convinced her he was not waking up. She wished she could go to sleep that easily. He had to be faking it, she decided.

Angie got out her blue notebook from her bag, making as much noise as possible. Phil kept sleeping. Cradling her pen between short fingers and not thinking of anything to write, she thought about drawing on Phil's face. Yeah, that's pretty immature, she decided.

She watched him struggle to wake up, before he dozed off

again. Angie wondered what a dinner date with Phil would mean. I hope I'm not doing it out of desperation. I don't like desperate people, she thought.

The back of the seat she faced seemed like it was staring back at her. She watched Phil try to wake up again. Yet, the train's click-clack, thump-thump sound was too lulling along with the side-to-side rocking movement. Angie wished she knew what he was dreaming about. She poked his arm until his eyes slipped open.

"What were you dreaming about? I read a book once about sleep. It said during sleep the brain's orientation is hyperaroused—neat word—and the brain generates false data about the body's location in space."

"I need a few more minutes of sleep before I can process and comment."

Phil's eyes blurred and closed. As the train switched tracks, his body shifted and his head dropped toward Angie. She shifted her shoulder toward him for support.

As his head fell against the soft part of her upper arm, his eyes twitched as if visiting the same dream. His mouth curled into a slight smile. Not a grimace of pain like he should be doing with his head at such a tilt. She decided he was dreaming about her. Let me have this, she told herself.

Angie looked down at her notebook and wondered how best to describe this Phil moment. She was all right with the discomfort in her arm. Cold and darkness passed her window and there was nowhere else to go at that moment, but to their station.

Phil rearranged his head so that his cheek fell more across her soft arm better. She reached up with her other hand and brushed away a lock of hair that had drifted onto his forehead.

After a few minutes, he opened his eyes, looked at her, and

smiled. Then he went back to sleep, leaning against her arm like a soft pillow. Angie stayed awake to make sure he got off at his stop. That morning she got on at an earlier stop to avoid her ex. Getting off at his stop would give him the opportunity to drive Angie to her car.

Train Commuter Waiting

For the last forty minutes, overhead announcements declared the evening commuter train would be there soon. Why didn't the automated voices admit the train was late and may never show up?

That's how the Commuter felt standing under the speakers listening to a mechanical voice he was tired of listening to. The noise overhead preyed on his worry as he got grayer, more tired, and just wanted to go home.

In front of him, the heated stagnant air flowed off the empty steel rails and seemed to pull his sweat and senses out of his frail self. Surrounding him, the mass of anxious commuters increased as people for the next train showed up to wait in the back of the waiting crowd. More sweaty people to sweat with.

The station was a transfer point where commuter trains out of the city could go south on one set of tracks or west on another. A few minutes later, the faceless announcements discussed the on-time arrival of the westward train as if the southern one had never existed. The Commuter stepped aside as people in the back left to ride on a different track home.

He could have left on this other westward train and lived

a different life. Yet, things would have been no different the next day. Just another commute from a different direction.

The Commuter just wanted to get through one more commute. Suffer through one more daily rite of passage to places he barely remembered because he was always commuting between them. If he could get through this commute one more time, he could do it all again tomorrow. Yeah.

Each morning, his commute started as he walked out of the house in the predawn darkness. He left his family in bed, not hearing his anguish. They lived a life he could afford as long as he commuted. This included his daughter's upcoming wedding.

"I don't want to dance with you at my wedding." The Commuter's daughter met him last night in the foyer of the house they shared. Before he could put down his backpack and ask why, she walked away. He did not get the chance to say how much he liked to dance.

In the kitchen he made a tuna sandwich and heated canned tomato soup for supper. When the Commuter sat down to eat, his wife came in and said, "I told your daughter you were a poor dancer."

"Why would you tell her that? I want to dance with my daughter at her wedding," said the Commuter. "After all, I'm her father."

"It's your daughter's wedding. She'll dance with whoever she wants to. She's thinking about dancing with her future father-in-law. He's a wonderful dancer. You can still walk her down the aisle as long as you don't trip." She dumped a splash of white wine into a coffee cup.

"Why would I trip?"

"You could be tripping all over the place and we'd never know since you're always commuting."

"I'm commuting to pay for everything we have, including this wedding."

"Then you should be thankful we're giving you a reason to commute," she said, leaving with her wine.

The Commuter got a cold beer from the fridge and it made the sandwich and soup taste better.

More train announcements jolted him back into his current commuting dilemma. The loud and taunting speaker above him claimed "other train movement" was responsible for his late train. These "other trains" pulled a menagerie of freight cars passed him on their given schedule. He wanted to know why his train could not be an "other train" since people were like freight.

The Commuter stood on the station platform considering that maybe his late train happened past a parallel universe and found a better way to commute, got sucked into a black hole and ceased to exist, or ran out of diesel.

He did not remember seeing a diesel carrying train to refuel other trains. Would the announcements say such things as black holes? Or admit there was a parallel universe with a better way to commute?

The Commuter felt an emptiness surround him. He wondered if he could sweat away to nothing and be remade into a different life where his train kept to a schedule and his family believed in him. Would it matter to anyone if my train never came, he asked himself? He wanted to escape from this commute and remembered when he was ten-years-old and first learned to dance. A twelve-year-old girl made him that confident.

Those many years ago on the Friday afternoon school bus, Amanda sat with her older friends while he read his *National Geographic* magazine alone. At the last bus stop, Amanda and he got off and walked together a block away to his aunt's house. This was where their parents would later pick them up after work.

Along their walk, she listened to him talk about his magazine. He wanted to be her hero when she said how her older friends ignored her. On his aunt's front porch, an FM radio played top-forty songs. His aunt's ginger snaps and lemonade got them talking about who they wanted to be one day.

"I want to travel around the world," said Amanda. It was a warm Friday afternoon with a tall elm nearby giving them cool shade.

"There's a lot to see out there," replied his aunt. She sat on her rocker doing her knitting.

The future commuter said, "Monday I'll bring some of my *National Geographics* so you can see the places you could travel to in the world."

"I'd like that a lot," said Amanda, smiling.

A pop song about teenagers in love filled the air. Amanda smiled more and twirled around on the porch like a ballerina. With the song playing on the radio, she reached out her hand to dance with him.

Passing cars honked and people waved. It was the first time he held a girl. He would always remember her smell and how she held his hands as they swung around on the porch. When the song was over, she told him what a great dancer he was and invited him to the Saturday school dance. Her smile meant nothing would stop him from that dance.

The next morning, he practiced in front of his bedroom mirror while Amanda went with her friends to the train tracks.

No one knew why the girls went there. Maybe it was to watch the heavy freight trains come by like thunder. In the end, it did not matter. It was a quiet, fast moving passenger train that caught Amanda standing on the tracks trying to be noticed by her older friends.

He wished he could have been a hero and saved her. Except, his only heroism was visiting her closed casket in a wood-paneled room with bleached curtains at tall, thin windows. The funeral home looked like it needed a funeral for itself. He left with a laminated explanation of her life that did not mention him.

For the rest of that school year, he walked to his aunt's place alone. She stayed in the house complaining about the heat, leaving the future Commuter sitting on the porch swing alone. The radio stayed off as he sat there remembering the dance.

The childhood memory rushed away from the Commuter as he stood waiting for his train with sweat stinging his eyes. He decided when he got home he would tell his family he was more than a paycheck and would demand to dance with his daughter at the wedding. He had let the commute separate him from his family. They had forgotten who he was.

"I'm living three lives. One for home, one for work, and one for this commute. That's three lives with the commute winning every time. This commute has become my sole existence. Do any of you hear me?"

Waiting commuters ignored him as if he did not exist. They were more worried about why the train refused to come.

"I won't be imprisoned by this endless commute anymore," he announced to the steel tracks before him.

More people arrived in the back of the crowd and he worried about being in front of so many anxious people. Thinking it was probably cooler in the rear and no longer important to be first on the train, he stepped away from the platform's yellow edge.

He kept moving toward the back of the crowd, feeling his hope of getting home dying. The Commuter kept moving backward until coming to the end of the commuting crowd where he stood under blue metal awnings. With sweat and frustration, tired legs and hurting back, he heard children giggling.

Another train came and went to places he did not want to go. Other passengers came and went. The Commuter edged further under the blue metal awnings toward the children's laughter. It was a wreck of a commute, anyway.

He closed his eyes and fell deeper into the memory of a lonely boy who had learned to dance and had no one to dance with. Somewhere he sensed the barren steel tracks and hot concrete platform fall further away until replaced with fresh, cool air running across a wooden porch. His headache and frustration faded as he opened his eyes.

In the distance, like a fading star, he listened to the short toot toot of a late train that would take him home. He let some other commuter simply replace him, or maybe not. It didn't matter. On the front porch of his favorite aunt, the FM radio played, a cool breeze from an elm tree took the heat away, and the sun showed everything clear and real.

He sat on a swing with Amanda, who stood and took the hand of a ten-year-old boy for his first dance.

About the Author

For over twenty years, I lived three hours a day, barring delays and mishaps, on a commuter train from home to work and back again. On the train, I had plenty of time to write about the people sitting around me who stressed up for work or school in the morning and unwound on the way home in the evening. *Evidence of a Commuter Train* captures my experiences of commuting by train.

I hope you enjoyed *Evidence of a Commuter Train*.

My blog is www.stanleybtrice.com.